on the sec... ...g.
*My co-pro... ...er
Gabrijela had arrived at
the start of the week to
prepare; also the
cast, who were busy
hawking other projects,
about which I was
both curious and
jealous. It's hard
to think of actors, good
actors, as anything
other than your
own once you've
worke... ...them.*

.

DIARY OF
A FILM

ALSO BY NIVEN GOVINDEN

We Are the New Romantics
Graffiti My Soul
Black Bread White Beer
All the Days and Nights
This Brutal House

DIARY OF A FILM

A FILM

NIVEN GOVINDEN

dialogue
books

DIALOGUE BOOKS

First published in Great Britain in 2021 by Dialogue Books

10 9 8 7 6 5 4 3 2 1

A CIP catalogue record for this book
is available from the British Library.

ISBN 978-0-349-70071-7

Typeset in Bembo by M Rules
Printed and bound in Great Britain by Clays Ltd, Elcograf S.p.A

Papers used by Dialogue Books are from well-managed forests
and other responsible sources.

Dialogue Books
An imprint of
Little, Brown Book Group
Carmelite House
50 Victoria Embankment
London EC4Y 0DZ

An Hachette UK Company
www.hachette.co.uk

www.littlebrown.co.uk

The point is not to direct
someone, but to direct oneself.

Robert Bresson

1.

I flew to the Italian city of B. to attend the film festival in late March. Our entry into the competition, a liberal adaptation of William Maxwell's novel *The Folded Leaf*, had been officially confirmed, and I was expected to participate in three days of interviews and panels to promote the release, with a jury screening on the second evening. My co-producer Gabrijela had arrived at the start of the week to prepare; also the cast, who were busy hawking other projects, about which I was both curious and jealous. It's hard to think of actors, good actors, as anything other than your own once you've worked with them. I knew they would be expecting me to see their films while I was there, wanting their betrayals to be blessed, and I anticipated that it would hurt as much as watching them with other lovers; a feeling especially pronounced when the new film was still warm on my lips. Eight months had passed since the production had wrapped and I missed their company, particularly the two leads, Lorien and Tom, who had a youthful ease that blended seamlessly into our production family. Nothing of the film could be changed at this point and I had made my peace with it, absorbing the heightened pressure of meeting strict deadlines in order to screen in this competition. There were other festivals through the spring and summer, but this was the one that mattered to me, having previously brought me luck and with it a sense of calm. But for all my confidence I arrived in the city feeling apprehensive. The trip had the air of both a working holiday and a funeral. There was excitement for the next stage in the film's journey, one in which I envisioned only good things, but also a finality, for with it my participation would cease. It was for Gabi, the actors and their publicists to take the baton and run for the glory they dreamed of. I could return to my home town of S., regroup, and retreat into my ideas. My first impulse on arriving at the airport was to have the car take me directly to the hotel, so keen was I to see Lorien and Tom again, to hear their voices and to feel their breath. I wanted to suffer their tender, respectful mockery, typical of young Americans who had been brought up well, but I was also aware that this would be the last time that I would play their loving God, and I wished to delay that. They had not yet seen the completed film so therefore a realm existed where they could not be disappointed in me. It wasn't the first time that I explicitly sought the love of my actors. There's an almost supernatural aura of openness, risk-taking and safety present in the shooting of some films that does not exist in others.

As always we had been pressured by a tight shooting schedule and insufficient money, but *The Folded Leaf* was
nourished by magic. It informed the breaking-light-of-
dawn shooting and held its power over us until the end of
the day. Drunk on its potency, it interrupted my sleep for
much of the principal photography, so keen was I not to lose
this holy atmosphere, fearing the mist would clear on
waking. I am not a superstitious man – there is no room for
the Ouija in filmmaking – but we were all touched by the
same feeling, and simply wished this gift to stay. It was
something I hoped was honoured in the final cut, and by
which Lorien's and Tom's faith in me would be justified, as
mine already was with them. I asked the driver to take me
to the harbour where the fishermen were delivering their
catch, with the strict instruction to collect me at the same
spot in half an hour. My late grandparents lived in a fishing
village, so there was something resolutely familiar in watching the boats come in. Fishermen from the one trawler
docked carried a procession of buckets to a line of trestle
tables holding large polystyrene boxes loaded with ice. I was
taken back to childhood and the surprise of seeing what was
there, watching now as the buckets were swiftly upturned,
a shower of fish clattering in their new ice boxes. Then, as
now, there was something depressing about being unable to
compete with nature, and how much of its infinitesimal
wonder could outsmart the camera. My film was set in the
Italian countryside, and though the gardens were lit by
angels, the fruit trees fulsome and glowing, they did not

contain the life that tumbled before me. I thought of parental disappointment when a child follows a lesser path, only the state of the film was entirely down to my hands; I was no bystander, but responsible for all of it. The woman on the other side of the table was shouting at me for blocking the view of others who were waiting to buy. I was awake then to the laughter of the grounded fishermen as they sluiced the blood and guts from the cobbles with buckets of fresh seawater, and the attack cry of the gulls that hovered above. Get a move on, came one man's voice. What's he doing? asked another. Make your decision somewhere else, mate. I seemed to move further back into the crowd, but I knew that I would not leave without buying a fish, eventually taking what was left in the box, a grouper and a sickly looking grey mullet, and going back to find the car. The bag was of the thinnest white plastic, gossamer to the touch, which allowed the rough texture of the grouper's scales to graze my palms as I walked. I could have held the bag by its flimsy handle, but instead, I held out the package horizontally before me, as if making an offering to anyone who would stop and acknowledge my presence. My film was offered on similar terms. By walking into the hotel and the suite reserved for my first meeting with Gabi and the cast, and then subsequently with journalists and potential distributors, I too was making an offering, as pure and sincere as the catch turning rigid in my hands until I suddenly felt embarrassed, dumping the package in the gutter before we drove away. I looked at my gesture rotting in the sun until it was out of sight, hoping the gulls would sense that it was there and quickly destroy the evidence. Talons tearing through plastic to reach flesh and bone; pecking and chewing until nothing remained. The hotel, a grand palazzo converted in the early sixties, always felt like home. It was a repository for both my successes and my failures; rooms where I had celebrated with abandon or cried bitter tears when the work was misunderstood. Once I stepped into the lobby and made myself known the process would begin, unstoppable in its certainty and form. I had no memory of why I wanted to make this film, what impulse had driven me to push this project above all other contenders, or what it was in Lorien's and Tom's previous work which had spoken to me of their potential as leads. I was unable to pinpoint the hour of shooting when I first saw magic and was compelled even more to push through, so sure of the story I was telling; fearful, of course, but determined. If anything, I wished to run from it. I knew of an espresso bar a short walk away, where I could drink coffee at an outdoor table, smoke a cigarette, and give myself some final space before the onslaught, and in walking I felt a purpose regained. It was tucked deep in the backstreets where the district changed into a working hue, an important factor in me wanting to go there, for to be away from the tourist throng was to be among the living. In finding the place I grew more certain of myself. I heard the strength in my voice as I caught the barista's eye and ordered a double; assurance in my posture as I leaned forward slightly, my palms lying flat on the counter. The craving for a cigarette did not fade but I was aware of the corrosive effect it would have on my voice, which needed to hold up for hours of interviews. I took my cup and found a space in a broken line facing the road, where it was possible to inhale the smoke of those sun-chasing customers: two men in their seventies, and a woman closer to me in age, middle fifties, each in their own space, minding their business. The sanctity of the smoker and the beauty of neighbourhoods, of pals and famil-iarity; the satisfaction of being in your corner of the world. I fought to have my film edited in my home town of S. as I had done with previous films, but the new financial backers had insisted I worked in a larger city, vetoing the expense of shipping prints and other masters from labs and sound studios to the set-up I had spent years building. I lived for three months in a nondescript apartment block ten minutes' walk from the edit suite, a mostly business district that turned to a ghost town in the evenings. Twelve weeks of regimen, forensic and all-consuming, away from my family for longer than I would've liked, in an artificial environment where the pleasure of gentle neighbourhood repetition was cast aside for something greater. This was working life, one which I was used to, only I had felt more withdrawn than before; a mixture of my lonely domestic arrangements and the luxurious sterility of my setting. Standing outside here eclipsed the blue of the edit suite; the silence that could be found through a city's white noise, the simple pleasure of coffee, with dappled sunlight hitting your face. This was where prosperity lay, not in the artificial nature of what I had filmed and submitted to the festival jury. I had to stop thinking this way: I'd made something beautiful but was struggling to accept this simple truth. Not for the first time; I'd had difficulty throughout my life with this. Do you want a cigarette? the woman asked. I have one here if you need. Am I making it that obvious? I said. I'm trying to be good, but the smell always gets the better of me. Ah! You're an ex-smoker! There's a saying that there's no one worse than one who's reformed, she said. In which case, I am profoundly guilty, I said. The woman was of a similar height and held my gaze as she spoke. When she reached into her pocket before holding a crumpled cigarette carton before me, she laughed, but in a way that was gently conspiratorial rather than disparaging and judgemental. She looked capable of that, too, in the flash of her eyes as a trail of teenagers on scooters thundered past, but in our interaction she was a nicotine comrade-in-arms; it was an international code that I had relied on many times over the years to break the ice. I could've spent the day at this spot, alternating between a bar stool at the counter and catching what sun there was outside. I felt something toxic being drawn out of my system the longer I stayed there, my mood lifting, fears waning. The woman was good company, and we covered everything from the price of coffee to the gentrification of the city. We talked of the lack of street signs in the area and how that was both a curse and a blessing, keeping the tourists away, but also creating difficulty for those genuine guests of the vicinity. My mother is a very proud woman, she told me. When she came to visit my new apartment she walked in circles for over an hour rather than ask a stranger for help with directions. We lamented the spiralling graffiti though we appreciated the art of it, and the city's failure to tackle the mountain of dog shit. I had a boyfriend in the eighties who was a graffiti artist, she said. He was one of those lost kids who wanted to disrupt. Disappear all night, and in the morning you'd hear of a new wall being covered in the city. He wasn't one of the vandals you see now, those kids on bikes who tag their names or stupid slogans on the shutter of their local pharmacy or whatever. He was an artist without the knowledge or means to break into art. The streets were all he had. What happened to him? I asked. Some of the guys in New York and London who were doing that became superstars, no? He killed himself, she said. He was closer to his paintings than I thought. Preferred being in darkness. I'm sorry to hear that, I said. It was a long time ago, she replied. Another life. I can show you where a couple of the murals still exist, if you're interested. She spoke with bravado to show that she had moved past her grief, but a shine in her eyes indicated how much the work still meant to her, and her incipient need to keep it remembered. I accepted immediately, from both curiosity and a sense that something greater would come from the invitation, whether in terms of the art or the ease of the woman's company. My nervousness as a child had made a nervous adult. It had taken me until my mid-twenties to learn how to cast this aside;

how my filmmaking would never flourish until I lost my shyness and was open to possibilities beyond the security of a film set. If a stranger asked you to see something new, you went without question, even if terrified. Finding the courage to talk to people who interested you, romantically and in other ways. You learn these things as you grow comfortable in your own skin, but for me it was a conscious process to leave the safety of my head, and I was unexpectedly reminded of this in the woman's offer. The opportunity had not presented itself in a long while. Or another time if you're not sure, she said. Just giving you a chance to escape in case you've changed your mind. I have no idea what your plans are for the day. You look as if you're expected somewhere else. What gives you that impression? I asked. You're the only one here wearing a suit, she said. That's not to say that no one owns a suit here. We're not savages. But yes, the cut of your suit, and the fact that you keep looking at your watch. A man who's either missed an appointment or is planning to miss one. It's all the same to me. I won't take it personally. I'm inundated with offers. She was neither sour nor frosty as she spoke, just straightforward with a dry sense of humour which made me like her even more. It was something the younger actors had to learn, to not take themselves so seriously. In my production company there was no room for hesitants, and in that regard she felt like a kindred spirit. I could almost see her working there, even though I knew nothing about her. We dinosaurs need to stick together, she said. Show these hooligans that they're not the only ones who know how to live. In leaving the bar, she offered her hand to reflect the business nature of our transaction. I'm Cosima. When I attempted to reply she cut me off with a smile and gentle wave of her wrist. I know who you are, she said. We have televisions in these parts, maestro. We visit the cinema. You're not so bad, raising her eyebrow as she spoke. Not so bad. I laughed in a way I hadn't for a while. We left the bar and walked along the narrowing street which squeezed traffic out completely, and through a residential square flanked by a domed church and a butcher's shop. The heart of Italy in twenty metres, she said, stretching out her arms. Prayer and blood. And food, I said. Yes, that too, she replied. This is a country that is never far from its guts. Past the butcher was an alley that wound behind the back of the church and its small graveyard – bones piled upon bones – and from there down a row of steps that led to a longer road. We were moving away from the residential area, towards the domain of garages and workshops, abandoned factories and boarded-up office blocks. In time, this too would be cleared, adding to the myth of the city – a reflection of the modernity it wished to embody, as well as the romance of what was left behind. We live in a medieval picture book, she said. You of all people should appreciate that. It's why I enjoy coming here, I said, but this is more than a museum. The city has a pulse, you can feel it; the tensions and contradictions inherent in living somewhere with so much history. It's a zoo, she said. And we're the animals. Everybody gaping as you go about your business. You're having a row with your lover on the way to work and everyone takes pictures, because a pretty girl crying on a bridge is the European cliché. You go for an eye appointment but you can't get into the doctor's office because a tourist has vomited on the front step, the handle and, somehow, the doorbell. So much beauty, so little time. Again, the raised eyebrow, and my prolonged laugh. She was special, this woman. We walked along a road of dead factories: hats, shoes, belts; the former pride of the city swallowed by larger global concerns, leaving in their place penury, nostalgia and the search for a new way of doing things. I almost heard the roar of the sewing machines and felt the noxious heat of the tanneries. My ears rang with the din of holes being punched through leather, of being studded with rivets or other decoration. I heard the slap of belt buckles on workshop tables and the gossip that passed between workers in their break room. She had taken me to a film set which was still very much alive. It's not much further, she said. His mother used to work in one of these buildings as a machinist, so he was always hanging around here. Before he started doing graffiti, he used to sketch the factory skyline. Heaven above, hell below, he called them. Standing with our back to the road and the workshop frontage facing us, varying in size, some grander than others even in their dilapidation, I traced their outline with my fingers, as if this was the last opportunity to commune. For the artists of my generation, coming of age in the late seventies and early eighties, all our parents had come from these places. It was our common ground.

The picture was a holy one: the din and a prayer. He'd take you here? I asked. We met here, she nodded. Bruno and I. I had a job between my studies packing gloves into boxes. He used to hang around outside waiting to walk his mother home. Then there was a day when he wanted to walk me home, so that's how it happened. Us. How does it make you feel to walk past these buildings? I asked. I too still lived and worked in my home town, where monuments denoting success and failure assailed me at every turn. The public toilets where I first had the courage to explore my sexuality with others; parks and cafe tables where I had declared my love; cinema aisles where I had cried about them afterwards. Train platforms and airport hallways: the totems of my escape and of passions lost. My triumphs and heartaches were architecture, both inescapable and invisible depending on my frame of mind. We've already walked past the place because I didn't want to point it out, she said. I try not to look for it. Reminds me of picking a wound. Wounds heal, I said, knowing this to be false, but feeling guilty of being led somewhere she didn't want to go. I have to pass this way at least once a week whether I like it or not, she said. I take tourists on guided art tours of the city. Depending on their taste, we may end up at one of the two murals. His work's been mentioned in a couple of books, but hardly anything exists to write about now. I do my part to keep him remembered. Creative acts should always be protected, I said. Good and bad. Otherwise how can the next generation learn? You're a lucky man, maestro, she said. You have an army of people to shine a light on your work. Here, I am just one person, with guided tours and a book that remains unfinished, may never be finished. You write? I asked, the words at last identifying the essence between us. More than survivors of draconian phases in post-war European history, more than ageing punks or new wavers who had fought for democracy through art and protest and any technologies we could find, who made their dissent known by speaking out or standing by the sides of more courageous brethren, our common ground was that we were both artists, with a deeply felt need to create work in order to survive. I sit at my desk but nothing comes of it, she said. I've been sitting at my desk for years. Pen scratching on paper. Notebook after notebook filled. What happens to it? Who knows? I'm waiting for a day when I feel a greater strength in my hand. A force that gives me the courage to pull the threads from all the writings into a coherent book that is respectful of his talent and what we had. And you've written about other things? I asked. Of course! She laughed. I'm not deranged, she said. Holding a candle like some Queen Victoria. I wear black because once you've been a punk, you can't dress any other way. Black's our uniform, yes? So I've written stories, and a novel that no one cared for, and a book about a painter and photographer that people did care for, but these things were many years ago. Now I write for art magazines and museum brochures. My uncle left me an apartment which I sold a few years ago, so that's enough. And you have the guided tours, I said. Yes, exactly, she said. It forces me to

leave my desk and venture outside. To breathe the air, con-
verse, show hospitality, all those things. I did it as a favour
for one of the museum trustees who had a guest in town,
then I repeated it for another colleague, and word started to
spread. I have a website now and all that nonsense. We look
at buildings, civic and public art, permanent collections, if
that's what they're interested in, as well as some of the private works. I know a few people in the city who will let me
show their treasures if I ask nicely. But not always the
murals? I asked. No, she said. Those I play by ear, depending
on their interest and attitude. If I show them other graffiti,
on the subway and suchlike, and they're dismissive, then I
know to give the murals a wide berth. They deserve more
than a cursory glance and a phone picture. At the end of the
factory row the road twisted again, and we found ourselves
on a narrow residential street, a line of skinny, turn-of-the-
century apartment blocks, the tops almost appearing to
touch in the small space, where sunlight worked hard to
penetrate shadow. It was incredibly claustrophobic after the
expansive space of before. I felt the darkness and anxiety of
so many people living overhead. He lived here with his
mother, she said, pointing to a block at the intersection of
the street with a wider road. Fourth floor. A bedroom for
his mother, and the sofa for him. There's talk of tearing these
down when they start clearing the factories but it hasn't been
decided. We walked towards the apartment block, slowly,
as if negotiating the cramped space. There was no one
around, adding to its oppressiveness, and challenging all

disbelievers that the genesis of great art could be found here. We've arrived, she said, key in hand. The eyebrow again. I thought you said it was a public mural, I said, confused. I did, she replied, it's in a public place. Why, are you nervous going into an apartment block with a strange woman? Not at all, I said, but for some reason I thought of my husband and child and whether I was giving them reason for further disappointment. It was unspoken, but both felt that I had not fought hard enough to edit the film at home; that there was something of the gypsy in my foundations which could not be tethered. They were believers in sleeping in the same bed every night and for me to do the same. Disorientation rippled through the house whenever I was away for extended periods, with each having to work harder to fill the lack. I felt this as deeply as they, driven by work, but restless and unhappy in my downtime; all the pockets that remained hidden from them, and kept out of my eyes and voice on our nightly FaceTime calls, or with greater effort on the weekends when they visited. Maybe we were all in a similar state of pain and compromise, brought on by a distance of several hundred miles, but for my part, I hoped that they were mercifully unaware. She opened the entrance door and walked me through the hallway, deserted of life, no mail or concierge, the footsteps solely ours. There was no detritus or voices to indicate occupation, but no dust or neglect either. It was clean but bare. She waved her hand with the assurance of occupancy. Developers are buying up these blocks one at a time in readiness for when the factory redevelopment begins, she said. They're all looking five, ten years into the future. No one has the permission to demolish anything yet, but it's common sense that the more property they own will give them a stronger hand. The city wants to erase their ghost towns. They want the streets filled and prosperous, and they'll do what's needed to achieve that. And they own this one? I asked. I was confused about the key and at her ease in the place. Empty buildings were my stock-in-trade, but the coldness of this one gripped hard on my shoulder from the moment we entered, as if she had unknowingly opened a door on to her own sorrow. Not yet, she said. This particular building and the one next door are owned by a family of four children who cannot agree on anything, so while they bicker and plot against each other, I still have some freedom to get in. We crossed the tiled floor and then up some concrete steps leading to the central staircase and a wider space beyond. We're going into the garden, she called. It was raining a few days ago, so I hope the ground isn't too soft. She led me past a paved area where a small table was upended against the wall with two chairs. I brought those, but no one's said anything, she said. There's a caretaker in the basement who keeps things presentable, and accepts my weekly processions. Ah, so the table is for your guests, I said. And for me, she replied. Guests or not, I can sit here for an hour or so and look at the mural on good days. It's there, can you see it? She pointed to the wall that bordered the scrub of grass before us, a pitch of maybe fifty metres, shielded in part by a cluster of pear trees, and a carpet

of ivy on the neighbouring wall. I pay the caretaker every
month to keep that at bay, she said, pointing to the ivy. I
have dreams that I'll turn up one day and the whole thing
will be covered by tendrils and leaves. This still may indeed
happen, I said. This is something you must accept.
Filmmaking had taught me much about finality; how the
obsession of a shoot, the freedom and pressure, friendships –
or at least the tenor of them at that particular time – all
ended. Living was learning to deal with endings in a way
that did not hurt you more. The scope of the mural was
evident from this distance; something of its form, how it
curled outwards from its originating point at the far left, a
tornado or cyclone, either trapping or expelling the best and
worst of humanity, or what could be ascertained of it from
the mind of a twenty-year-old child. From a black background, an unknown universe whose energy force was
without measure, it swirled into our domain, and into it fell
dancing girls, fireside babies and their newspaper-reading
parents, gangsters holding up cars, and gap-toothed women
rolling out pasta on kitchen tables. There were smoking
monkeys, and aristocrats with their pants down; fishermen
pulling on snagged lines, boom boxes pumping out gloves
and belts rather than musical notes, and a jam of cars trailing
into the abyss. All emanating from a cloud morphing with
time into a plume of smoke, which led to the faintest linear
scrawl along the bottom. The skyline of the factories and
the ecosystem there. It was the life from this building and
those nearby, transposed and commented on in the dead of

night, over weeks, months. It was extraordinary. It was the heads that were the most striking, geometric blocks that only featured the eyes and mouth, the details concentrated solely in the actions and situations. It separated them as individuals while at the same time bringing them together: his people of the neighbourhood, and all the contradictions of the wider city. He did all this is in spray paint? I asked. The precision he has! His hand! I don't know what I'd been expecting, feeling too warm and distracted by the depth of our conversation and from the pleasure of simply walking with someone you found agreeable. I had stopped thinking about what the paintings could mean, and the resonance they may hold. I was floored by the detail of it, and by the fact that the hands which created it were no longer here to create again. The world would not change on seeing this, but it was more than the work of a bored teenager. Its critical eye, its humour, needed to be seen. It pleases you? she asked. There was a note of childish hope in her voice, betraying the cool of her posture as she sat at the newly opened table and smoked a cigarette. I had moved closer to the mural to examine its detail, looking for signs of one idea leading to another; not so much the genesis I was after but more the sequence of events. It comes from an editor's mind, the mindset I still had on just completing the film. I was forever looking for joins. I pressed my fingertips into the wall, and then my hands. I wanted to feel the texture of the brick through the paint, as well as the sheen of the spray cans themselves. I was guided by touch, the essence of what drove

this boy, his wonder and anger. There are some similar
sketches on paper, she said. Most are in black marker and a
few with charcoal when he was conscious that he should be
working the way 'artists' should. He got a box of slate from
one of the old-timers in the workshop in exchange for delivering his lunch for a week. The guy thought he was crazy.
To him, it was just old crap they had lying around; as familiar, necessary and hated as family can sometimes be. Why
don't you buy some nice expensive pens? I remember him
saying. If you want to draw well, you'll need pens instead
of this rubbish. But I'm a drawer of rubbish, is what Bruno
replied. Like for like. So he thought of himself as an artist,
I asked, and not just a graffiti guy? He was starting to, she
said. Before the end. Not something he discussed, more
coming out during instances when he was asked. The first
time I heard him say it was then, when we went to collect
the slates from the old man, and I thought, Yes, you are. Just
that simple definition made sense of his passion and his habit
of disappearing. It made me happy because I realised that I
understood him. In speaking, her expression had flowed
from pained to contented, at peace with her conclusions.
Her truth was the acknowledged one, affirmed by her boy,
so this was why she had no regrets. I envied her. My family
were my truth, but there were others during the making of
films that could not be denied. The fire that came from
creating work and the moths that flew into its orbit. Those
beautiful, occasional moths that would derail me. The
sketches were lost also? I asked quickly, for a flash memory

from set pulled at me suddenly, and I needed to be drawn away from the thought before I cried out. It had been an early moment when Lorien and Tom had looked at me with such clarity in the seconds before we shot a scene, and how that was transmitted in the minute of action that followed. They were in a diner drinking their coffee and talking of very little which was outwardly important, but something in their emotional literacy clicked. They understood themselves and their characters in ways they hadn't before. Each had long thought of himself as an actor, now they were understanding who they were as artists, enabling us to speak silently in that moment. Just those few seconds was all it took to set the overall tone of the film, and I could never forget the power of that. His mother gave me all the sketches, she said. She didn't know what to do with them. I think their physical presence in the apartment was too painful. She had her photographs to worship, a shelf of albums above an altar she made. But the drawings. There was too much life there, too many fires. Don't get me wrong, she talked about his art to whoever would listen. Her pride in her son was as consuming as her grief. She would drag people to the back garden to this mural, and the railway tracks on the outskirts of the grand station where the larger work remained. She made people take photographs. She bossed and bullied them towards which sections to give attention to, and to pay respect to its scope. He brought the personal to a place you thought of as impersonal, a shitty wall that bordered the rail tracks. His mother could handle this. But the sketches, she said, falling silent. I closed my eyes and imagined the gentleness of his hand as he worked from the sofa or the kitchen table. The tenderness of those memories must have been too much to share. Maestro! She had collected herself. Come and sit down, she said. You've been standing on the wet ground for too long. Winter's over, I know, but I can still feel the chill. I don't want to be blamed if you return to wherever you need to be with a cold. They'll string me up. I went and sat across from her, took the cigarette offered and puffed at it weakly. You've gone very pale, she said. I'm not sure whether that's down to the outdoors or what you've seen. I'm presenting a new film, I said, at the festival. I'm a dinosaur who still prefers to shoot and edit on film, and sometimes I'm lucky enough to get my own way. I'm still trying to process how I feel. And it has nothing to do with pride? she asked. Because I have a feeling that you take pride for granted, for to complete every film must be an achievement in itself. Look at me and my book! Scraps after scraps. You have nothing to worry about, maestro. Present your film and feel sure of yourself. It's not always that simple, I said. Working with actors doesn't necessarily make me a good one. I find it difficult to lie. What is there to lie about? she said. You wouldn't say a film is complete if you didn't believe it. Instead, you're in purgatory and are fighting to accept it. That's no cause to be miserable. Take heart from those who wish you well, because you'll be surrounded by many champions tonight, I'm presuming. The maestro and his lions! Let those who want to attack attack. You have your film and nothing else matters. It was as strident a defence as I had heard for a long time. It was years since even one of my collaborators had mounted such a passion. When you find those with a talismanic quality, whose outlook aligns with yours, you must be wise to their value and find a way to hold that person close. How to explain this to Cosima in words that were not foolish? We had walked for two hours and in that time everything had changed. Instead, I said simply, You have faith where I have none. But this afternoon I will find it, dredge every rock and crevice until I find fragments to grasp. Climbing one step at a time until I feel my confidence restored. Until then, we walk? she suggested. Yes, I agreed. We walk. I looked at the mural for a final time before we left the garden while my guide finished her cigarette. It did not do justice to take pictures – an insult to the eye and heart – but I tapped repeatedly on my phone, moving from corner to corner until I had recorded everything in detail, and then, in rejoining Cosima on the terrace, I took a series of wide shots to capture the full length of the piece in situ. I knew that I would not return here and was compelled to record something should my memory fail me. The chairs, the blossom giving promise of fruit on the pear trees, the back of the apartment block itself, its decay evident in the blistered paintwork and peeling window frames, and Cosima's profile when she thought I was focusing elsewhere. I wanted a record of what I had seen and felt, as if I would need to prove someday that I was there. I thought you perhaps didn't believe in photographs, she said.

You took nothing of the factories or of the walk. I was enjoying the novelty of it. When I take my groups around, they spend more time playing with their phones than listening to what I say. I want to remember everything, I said, here. You understand? I do, she said. Come, there's one more place I want to show you before we leave. Is there still some energy in those legs? There is, I said, filled with a lightness I could not give a name to. Good to hear, it's a steep one so may test you. We walked the eight flights of stairs, four floors, to his old apartment. Two apartments on each floor; the communal space, as below, tidy and cold. Your first film, she said, with that famous shot of the young couple kissing on the tenth floor, with your camera in the lobby stairwell pointing up to reach them? We recreated that. Gave my camera to the woman who was the janitor at the time. Had a sharp eye, that woman. Sharp tongue, too, but she knew how to take a good picture. We used the space that ran through the middle of the stairwell, see? I had prints made for both of us. I'd like to see it, I said, knowing that it was as much for the composition of the shot as to see their young passion. It's lost now, she said. His mother may have his copy, but I have no idea. All I have is the memory of the place. Of doing it. Fourth floor, fifth floor, Bruno would say after that, whenever he wanted a kiss. Come here, 'Misa. Put your books down and give me some sugar. Fourth floor, fifth floor. You have a key to this also? I asked. No, she said. This is my only failing. When his mother left the city, the apartment once again became the property of the landlord. The

caretaker has all the keys, but to ask for access is to broach
a line neither of us wants to cross. There is turning a blind
eye in the garden and there is being complicit in a greater
trespass. We are both fearful of the latter. You're writing a
book, I said. It's perfectly above board. She looked at me
steadily before replying, catching her breath so that those
extra seconds gave her time to formulate her words. It's how
I want it, she said. Avoiding temptation. There are details I
intend to omit from the books. Some memories need to be
just for me. I'm not so selfless as to destroy myself for the
sake of accuracy. She sat outside the door, her back against
the wall, and motioned me to do the same. This is my pro-
tection device, she said, tapping her foot against the frame.
A block of wood that stops me from going to pieces. Keeps
my mind sharp, too. I sit here and remember the two rooms:
the kitchen-living room, and his mother's bedroom behind
that. I think of his profile in the doorway, or his shape on
the sofa as he bent down to draw. Or my feet pushing against
the sofa's edge on the afternoons I would sleep there, when
his mother was still at work and I had called in sick. I
remember the light from the other apartments hitting the
ceiling on those afternoons. The two of us content to lie
there in darkness. I think of the acoustics of the hallway, and
how our laughter would ring – the anticipation of arriving
and the satiation in leaving. These are the things I need to
hold close. He painted in there too, didn't he? I said, as if it
had all become clearer. She nodded. On every wall. It was
one of the ways his mother tried to keep him at home, she

said. She was always so scared that he would get arrested, or worse, hit by a train when he was going back and forth across the tracks. And the work is similar? I asked. The need to know more was making me light-headed. I would take all the dizziness in the world to see another painting. I was frightened by the strength of the impulse and swallowed hard to lose it from my voice. After all you've told me, it seems unbelievable that there is still this unseen work. Most of it was work in progress, she said. Him trying things out that could later be seen elsewhere. But there are other details. Portraits of his mother. Portraits of me. When she said this, the torture in her face was plain. We had gone too far for her to hide it. I fear the vacuum in opening the door, she said, to find what I remember has crumbled to dust. The erosion of the public murals I can accept, however much it pains me. Their location, the elements; both are out of my control. The sanctity of the apartment, however. I should say that it's empty: all the furniture was removed after his mother left. It's not the objects I fear, or the lack of them. I fear the space itself, that by standing in an empty room, my memories will turn on me, one cancelling out another until there is nothing left. Does that sound mad? Anything but, I said. There are times when you must batter down the doors closed to you, but equally there are those doors that shouldn't be opened, or at least, opened with care. Do you truly believe that? she asked, and in her eyes confirmation that this was the right way to live. To survive. I do, I said. Art comes from imperfect places and its practitioners are as imperfect as the work they create. There is no right way. The truth in this was palpable. We stayed on the concrete floor and clung on to what felt real, the ghosts of the building and of promise lost. We silently acknowledged our respective faiths and embraced the coping mechanisms that allowed us to keep going. We held on to all this, and then, under the blessing of her past love, held on to each other.

2.

Returning to the hotel I assumed some of my responsibilities. I met with Gabrijela and went over the final schedule. The press panel would now take place before the screening tomorrow, leaving only one interview with a trio of influential film writers that evening which was imperative that I attend alongside the actors. In no uncertain terms she made it clear that everything hung on the critical reception at the screening. I had worked with Gabi since my first film, and she knew better than to lecture me, but it was telling that her time spent at the festival so far, networking and seeing other films, had set a pessimistic mood over our makeshift office. Save this foolishness for the actors, I said. You're telling me nothing useful. The climate around the festival this year . . she said, their buying patterns— This is just filling up empty air, I said, cutting her off more sharply than I liked. We make films without gimmicks, so they'll have to decide whether that's fashionable or not this year, I said.

Why force the issue when it's not your decision to make? All we can do is our job. You're in charge of filling the premiere with buyers, so make it busy. What's inside the canister is down to me. The print was awaiting my inspection, and I was bundled into a car that took me to the screening room ten minutes away from the hotel. It was where I had screened previous films, and on its approach I felt the force of conflicting emotions as I remembered both good times and bad. Gabi was right to prepare me. It was her job to keep me from walking naively into the competition when she had knowledge to share. She had read the runes and was nervous for our outcome. I was nervous also but realised that I would not be crippled by it. Whether this film played solely in this theatre or another thousand others, it existed in the world, shaped by my hand. As an artist this is all you can ask. Gabi's role as the businesswoman would be to ask for something else, but that was not solely my meter. I would not be ripped off for the price of the work when the distribution offers came in, but nor would I compromise for the sake of a higher bid. At the cinema I went directly to the top room where I shook the projectionist's hand, and answered her questions about the screening. As she prepared, I walked into the theatre and sat in the centre. There was a particular seat I always used for the process, both in the name of objectivity and as a charm. I was a man without superstition who still clung on to this particular seat. I texted Cosima and asked her if she wanted to see the film ahead of everyone else. You may be sick of me already, I wrote, but if you're not, I'd value your opinion. What happened to your lions? came the reply. The lions are sleeping, I texted back. The energy that pulsed through my hand as those texts were sent and received. We had parted only an hour since, in a bashful acknowledgement that our time spent walking had been an unexpected one. I was in a particular state of shock as I walked away, one where I was dazed but still somehow alert, my senses heightened, so that the steps back to the hotel felt new to me. I worried that she would think I only wanted her there as a placebo; that having made it clear that she supported my work, she needed to continue her affirmations during the screening. A maestro who did not exist without his sycophants. It was down to me to dispel that and for her to understand that she must speak her mind. Only the weakest of artists had to be told what they needed to hear, and I was cut from a different cloth. You'll have to rouse your lions, came her reply. I have to work this afternoon. Free from 6 p.m. if you still need another opinion. That was that. Three lines, friendly enough, which killed the dream. It stopped whatever was brewing and brought me down to earth. Work. The work. What was expected of me. We ran the first and last reel and nothing of my opinion changed. Picture and sound filled the theatre with the sensuality I'd hoped for; the performances themselves, luminous and truthful. People could decide what they wanted, but in that moment I was proud and content. When I returned to the top room, the projectionist stopped what she was doing and walked over to hug me. You've made something beautiful, she said, smiling. They'll lap it up, trust me. I was elated by her response, and also guilty. Was this what I had wanted when I summoned Cosima? Or something more? Vain, foolish man that I was. At the hotel I relayed this to Gabi, which seemed to restore the confidence that was lacking earlier. I wondered what it was that had made her so gloomy, but did not dwell on it. When the spirits of the company are up, you must work hard to keep them so, no matter the spiritual expense to yourself. We hugged it out and both breathed. In the privacy of my room I spoke to my husband and child and told them that I loved them. My son replied that I was being hysterical and went back to playing ball in the backyard. My husband was sorting laundry and did not have much time to speak either. Why are you ringing in the middle of the day? he complained. Are things going that badly wrong? Call back later. The normality of their rejections filled me with pleasure. I'd returned to my foundations, settled and ready for what would follow. I pulled off my shoes and lay on the bed, where I slept uninterrupted for an hour. It was as restful a sleep as I'd had since the final edit began. It was an all-encompassing blackness without anxieties or dreams. I fell into oblivion without fear of where I would land; the freedom of nothing, bar silence and warmth. When I entered Lorien and Tom's interview suite shortly afterwards, I felt restored and childishly eager to be reunited. The adoration required for your actors is immeasurable; the desire you must have for them. If you could not fall in love with your ciphers you were merely pushing chess pieces around a set, wooden and replaceable, reflecting all that was closed inside you. This was not in my nature, for my films needed to be flesh-and-blood realisations of what was on the page. I would fight for the people I wanted until I got my way. I flattered and protected them, giving all the freedom and encouragement needed to allow truthful performances to emerge. Lorien and Tom were babies, pliant but sometimes unwilling to dig as deep as necessary, and I was tough in those instances, asking for more in take after take, until they mined the reserves I knew they innately held. I never asked actors to give what I knew I could not. So while sometimes they may have felt the yardstick driving them, they surely knew that my faith in them came first, even if they were less aware of how it destroyed me afterwards. How consuming the attention to detail in the hours before and after they were on set; my passion expressed through lighting, honing the script, arranging and rearranging props, and later in the edit suite, brokering the silence between words and actions. Those bastards have torn you apart, my husband said, on seeing me when I returned home after shooting wrapped. They've taken everything but your flesh, and even that's in a sorry state. Only my husband knew what it took to build me back up; the patience needed to nurse me back to health. I had spent half of my career not knowing how to look after myself, crashing from film to film, and explaining away my sadness as one of the pitfalls of the job. I worked without significant breaks, fearful of what would happen should I stop: that either my name would be forgotten or my ideas would vanish into nothing. The pressure you put on yourself at a young age to keep going was something I wanted to shield my actors from. I encouraged them to think carefully about the parts they were offered and to be wary of taking on more commitments than they could handle. Pissing in the wind with the hungrier actors, but I tried. Look at the example I'm giving you, I wanted to say. There are only so many times that you can strip yourself away. A day will come when you will try only to find that everything you held has melted. Here he is! said the younger actor. Our genius has landed! I'd forgotten the feeling of Tom's arms around me, the involuntary laugh that came as I kissed his cheek; he wanted to touch but the Midwestern boy in his genes fought it, still learning continental ways. I hear you got sneaky this afternoon, he said, and had yourself a screening without me. Would've been down like a shot if I'd have known about it. I heard you were talking about your other movie all afternoon, I said, otherwise I would've called you. How did those interviews go, by the way? They seemed to like the film, he said, blush spreading across his cheeks, his Midwestern modesty. It's had two screenings since Tuesday. People are fighting to see it. Congratulations, I said. You must be happy. I am, maestro. I'll be happier when I see our collaboration, though. It's what I'm most excited for. It does you proud, I said. You'll see. I'll have to take your word for it, he said, for now. The trust in his eyes assailed me; the unconditional love of a child. He trusted me because I had not humiliated

him; how he had been listened to on set, pushed, praised.
He'd been made to feel safe, never criticised for trying, only
for perceived laziness, zipping through scenes when he was
tired and thought it would do. Through all this he had
grown, Lorien also. They were not the same young men
who'd arrived in Europe ten months ago. What they had
learned would not leave them, from packing and canning
fruit, to pressing olives, how to kiss another man on camera
and show their truth. I was emotional, for I knew that it was
simply another stage they had to pass. They would learn
from other directors and experiences and grow in new ways.
There was a connection between us that was lasting, but
those firsts could never be replicated, as their minds processed those rituals that were unknown to them. We hugged
again, and like all parents I swallowed it down, my mixture
of pride, love and the regret at time passing. Parenthood was
the tension between the exhilaration of the present and grief
for the past; the future too, both hoped for and feared. I
thought of my own boy and how his face would change in
even this short time away from him; his hair and nails
longer, and something different in his mannerisms whether
it was a new catchphrase or interest. I ached for my family
at home, to be rooted within them, but this was my family
too, whose needs could never be neglected. Where's Lorien?
I asked. He's upstairs getting a haircut. Been on a hippy vibe
since the film wrapped. Working on projects where he
looked like a bum. You wouldn't approve! Dress how you
want to dress, I said. The film's finished. I don't govern you

the way they do in Hollywood. You said it, maestro. It's down to his agent. She saw some pictures of him at the festival yesterday and hit the roof. Major burn, he laughed. He'll be the slickest dude you see tonight, but he'll hate every minute of it. Let's go for a walk instead of waiting around, I suggested. Yes please, he said. There's a crazy good coffee bar I found that made me think of you. I can't wait to see maestro's face when he tastes how good these espressos are, I was saying to Lorien. How so? I asked. They're as good as we had at your place, he said. Maybe better! You should see the machine they use. It's a beast! We took a car along the seafront and then through a maze of backstreets that bordered the Duomo. How did you find this place? I asked. A girl who's been translating for us, he said. We walked here the morning after last. I think her parents have a place nearby. The bar was modern in a rustic style of stripped floors and exposed walls, wooden beams and chic lighting. He probably had similar spots in New York and LA, and possibly one in the gentrified part of his Rust Belt home town, introduced to him by similar girls on similarly enchanted mornings. He was a young actor. Let him live this way. The coffee blend was sound, but the barista rushed the tamp, recognising Tom and becoming self-conscious. It tastes of chocolate, doesn't it, he said, and some kind of fruit that I don't know the name of. When I agreed he glowed with pleasure. In time, he would learn to hold back feelings from showing on his face, but this was now, and the beauty of it was overwhelming. He would become a better actor simply by learning how better to hide. No other director would capture the same essence because our summer could never return. I was both bullish and aggrieved by it. It's a busy time for you, and yet you look so relaxed, I said. I feel comfortable here, he replied. The noise. The smells. I come from a town of cornfields, a bowling alley and a cinema. It's a working town but everyone's asleep. Zombies harvesting the fields and preaching in church. I'm alive here, in a way that I don't feel in the US. It's like being switched on to a different way of doing things. My senses. Everything's in Technicolor, even the insults and dog shit. Remember that restaurant you took us to outside Genoa? Looked like a hut in the middle of nowhere. In the hills? I said. The place where we ate for literally five hours straight, he replied. Made us eat like proper Italians, rather than people who have to work out twice a day. This place made me think of the hut. Same integrity, even though it's a flashier spot. So you're feeling like a local now, I teased, knowing the good places from the bad. No, maestro, he said. More that I'm beginning to understand what travel does to me. How it shapes what I see. In my first meeting with Tom, he gave similar sparks of self-reflection and loathing. He was unafraid to show his sensitivity or his ignorance. He hungered for the script and the chance to make it real; bursting with ambition and open to possibility. I loved him from that first meeting and loved him now. I thought of drinking espresso with my son in the same bar when the time came, whether he would be so open; and wondered if he would look at me with guile or contempt. Was the power of Tom in that he would not judge me in the way my own child would ten years from now? I was cushioning myself for the reality I deserved, the reality all parents faced; running like a coward when I should've been at home with my flesh-and-blood boy. You think I came from this, I said, gesturing around. I made discoveries, same as you are now. The world is happy to stay closed to you if you let it. You'll not be satisfied with that, I can see. The espresso, making new friends in different cities. You're on quite an adventure. No more so than now, he said. Anyway, I'm happy that the three of us get to spend some time together these next few days. He was playful as he downed the remains of his cup. Let's take a stroll around the block before we head back, he said. Been cooped up in that rabbit hutch all day. Need to stretch my legs. We'll be late, I said. If we keep them waiting they'll be furious. Since when did you follow the rules, maestro? he said. The man who pulled his film the night before he was meant to show it? Who once punched a critic on La Croisette? We can sneak ten minutes. Do you have any cigarettes? I don't want you smoking, Tom, I said. When in Rome, man, he said. I've had one or two so far. Nothing I can't handle, so you don't have to look at me so disapprovingly! OK, I said, you make the decisions. I'm no policeman. I'll treat you to a pack. That's what I was hoping you'd say, he said. I didn't bring any cash with me, as usual. The coffee bar was converted from the ground floor of a townhouse, situated in a tree-filled square. It was overlooked by houses on three sides, with the wall from the structure on the neighbouring street enclosing it. The square itself was partly paved, and in its centre no more than a patch of scrubland where locals walked their dogs and couples met clandestinely when there were no other places to go. There was a statue of a general riding a horse which gave reason to the space, its name plaque, like the wall behind it, clouded with graffiti. We walked the perimeter twice under the general's gaze, two inmates on exercise duty, making the most of their allotted hour of fresh air. Tom grinned at me as he took long drags from his cigarette, happy that this was something else we could share, but at the same time challenging me to say something. I didn't. I'd seen his schedule for the week and knew how hard he was working; carrying these two films at such a young age and not buckling under the pressure. At twenty years old I was still daydreaming in my room, not knowing who I was. I would never have been so capable. These squares drive me crazy, he said. I think I find my dream house in every one I cross. His arm was loosely draped over me as we walked. His face was dreamlike but punctuated by seriousness. It was impossible not to see how the place filled him. He would never be an American as typically defined. He was changing and would continue to change. It's the hidden magic of cities like these, I said. They're willing you to be seduced. I come from a town similar to this one, but whose beauty escapes me in many ways. I hold too many grudges in each brick and rooftop. If you asked the people who live here they'd probably tell you the same thing. I hear that, he said. A magazine photographer came to my home town last year to shoot me for a cover profile, and she was getting all teary-eyed and philosophical about my parents' farm. If you knew the shit that went down on this farm, I wanted to tell her. The farm is still part of who you are, I said, same as me and my hated rooftops. Even if you never go back, its existence brought you here. What acting gave him was more than just the opportunity to escape. He was growing with every experience, soaking in his environment and choosing what to lose or keep. In two laps of the square alone, he seemed somehow changed. Again, it was something I both marvelled over and regretted, for my own opportunities for renewal were finite now, if they existed at all. Are you dressing Italian too? I asked. That scarf you're wearing probably has a story behind it. Very chic. Lorien bought it for me yesterday, from Gucci, he said. Was yanking my chain about how I should try and fit in with the locals in my new espresso bar. He was being snarky because he couldn't get his head around these fancy sneakers I was wearing that Vuitton sent me, but it's actually a pretty good scarf, right? Yes, I said, it's a good scarf. Your benefactor has taste. Don't say it so seriously, maestro, he laughed. That makes me nervous! How would you want me to say it? I asked. The same way, I guess, he said. I'm just anxious for your approval. Like I am with so many things. I trust your judgement the way that you trust mine, I said. Lorien was still not ready when we returned, finishing a phone interview in the neighbouring suite. We shouted our greetings through the door, needing to make him aware of our presence, but he did not reply. The playfulness and urgency in our voices; impatient for him to be within our orbit. So this is our cage, I said, gesturing around the suite; oppression in the comfort of the sofas and the floral arrangements; something of our humanity robbed in the table of snacks and soft drinks, and in the presence of the publicist sitting outside. Our behaviour to be monitored and regulated by our keepers; how we were expected to be word perfect and ready to perform the moment our guests entered. I felt the pressure of the set, the click of the camera turning over, how that rang through the silence, followed by the snap of the clapper, thunderous, like a gun being fired at close range. What will you say, I asked, in these interviews? Same as I've been saying all week, he replied. That this is the kind of part you wait for, with a director you wait for, and a co-star you wait for. The truth, in other words. I'll say that after this kind of film experience, a blessing in many ways, I'll be lucky to find myself in the same situation again. That there are other films happening, and further films after that, directors I want to work with and stories I want to tell, but that none will touch the magic of making this movie, either personally or professionally. I'll be the luckiest actor alive if it does. I'll be the only man who's been struck by lightning twice and lived to tell it. He was standing with his back to me, and in turning around as he finished speaking, I saw the brightness in his eyes, the conviction there. I'm not telling you anything you didn't already know, maestro, he said. I'd row the Atlantic single-handed for the chance to work with you again. I just need to make it plain to these folks. If you talk like that, I won't have to say anything, I began. I'll be lucky to get a word in. You're just being spiky because I told you honestly, he said. Accept the compliment in the spirit that we always accept yours. I do, I said. I'm still a little fried from finishing the edit. I'd forgotten how much the machine demands from you once the film is ready to view. It's honesty you have a problem with, maestro? No, never that, Tom, I said. It's more about how much you need to give of yourself. Mentally you'll be as spent as you might be on set. This is a set, of kinds, he said, just without the uncomfortable farm clothes. There are still lines to learn and marks to hit. Harder in a way, because you need to show yourself without giving too much away or finding yourself damaged by it afterwards. When I think about acting all I want is to strip myself away until all you see is the character. Interviews are a halfway version of that, only it's a strip without the anaesthetic. You don't have the luxury of being in a fog as you stand next to your scene partner and the cameras start to roll. You're wide awake and fighting harder to protect yourself. I find a way, though. Always find a way. But you show so much on your face, I thought. You are incapable of guile, until I realised a barely perceptible shift in his tone. He was no longer speaking to me as Tom in the local square. Tom, the actor was coming forward, honest and affable, but defined in solely their terms – the expectations of Gabi and our financial backers. I'd seen older actors

transform in previous junkets, but in more heavy-handed
ways: a series of exhalations and a toss of their mane in the
corridor outside before they stepped into the room. The
more spiritual of them requesting twenty minutes of alone
time in the bathroom without disturbance. Tom's change
was instant; it flowed with his breath and heartbeat. And as
if to challenge me, with the next pulse he was back to Tom
again, the one I truly knew, with nothing to hide. We're
going to get dinner after this, right? he asked. Gabi said there
was somewhere you wanted to take us that would blow our
minds. I know a little place, I admitted with a laugh. Just
what I wanted to hear, he said. Why do you think I've been
living on espresso and salads since I got into town? Been
saving myself for the pasta mountain facing us tonight. You
made the right preparations, I said. If you hurt tomorrow, I
don't want to be blamed for it. Ha! I'm ready, maestro, he
said. Bring it! If our bellies are bulging over the tabletop at
the panels tomorrow, then so be it. I could probably do with
getting a little thicker. How's Lorien in interviews? I asked.
As you'd expect, he said. He nails it. There's something in
sitting with someone who's been around a little longer. How
sharp he is. I've learned a lot, just from the few pre-
interviews we've already had this week. He gives me
confidence when I'm unsure about things. You gave me a
brother when you put us together for this film, you know
that, right? He'd say the same about you, I replied. Only in
a more grouchy way, Tom laughed. And that's OK, he said.
A grouch I can take, so long as he's mine. The air

conditioning picked up and with it the tension in the room
heightened. I felt a series of knots twisting through my
stomach, limiting blood flow and squeezing the life from my
vital organs. The first scene on a film, the same feeling: that
what had been endlessly planned for had finally arrived; how
what would follow was down to both the extent of that
preparation and what you held that was unknown. Lorien's
and Tom's first scene had been together and their prepared-
ness showed in their body language, in the nodded
affirmations as they took their marks, the wave of their heads
as the set was cleared. Just a flash in the eye contact between
them, in acknowledgement of their nerves along with their
willingness to fight for the other; brotherhood forming in
that moment, irretrievably blended so that they would not
break. Hey, maestro, you're starting to look tense, said Tom.
Lighten up! I'd say run a lap of the room or something, but
if we start getting all sweaty now the publicist will murder
us. They'll murder us anyway, I said. There's always one
thing or another that we'll forget or fluff up. You almost
sound scared of them, he said. These are people you hired,
after all. In this case, we hired them to be ferocious, I
explained, to us as much as everyone else. I told myself that
I was not scared but the fear would not dissipate. I was still
so exposed from the newness of the film. There had been
no time to grow a skin as my actors had, shedding something
of the farm as they went to work on other roles. For me, this
was all I had: one ship to helm and keep afloat. I was still in
the water while my captaincy was judged. All the logic I

could conjure paled in the strength of my primal responses, a reminder that what was cultivated had lesser strength than the blackness that festered deep in my marrow. The essence that had driven me to make films in the first place: a union of what I'd learned with what I felt. I breathed slowly, a reminder that fears could be harnessed if I collected myself. Life was a series of harnessing and unharnessing, riding and falling. In film I had fallen many times, yet I was still here. How dependable history was in the signs that it gave you. I accepted the fatalism of the moment. The three of us would talk of the film for the first time, and it would be the marker of how we spoke of it afterwards. It would be what it was, and looking into Tom's eyes, I nodded that I was ready.

3.

It was a good-humoured dinner underscored by gentle drunkenness; plates of primavera greens, cuttlefish and black rice, silken ribbons of pappardelle with wild hare, and curd cheese tarts, sweetened with honey and mascarpone. Gabi and our publicist had joined us, everyone elated with the first interview where the case for the film had been made, and not only accepted, but applauded. The three journalists present, who had seen a preview screening, were agreed that this was a story which needed to be told, and who were convinced beyond measure by its truth. One of those critics, who had famously walked out of one of my films a decade earlier, was moved to tears, and pulled me aside before leaving. Your problem has always been in how you find beauty in unexpected places: the factory, the docks, inside political office, and now on this farm, he said. We are not always ready for what you find, and that has never bothered you, which frustrates us even more. But your single-mindedness is also your greatest strength, that and your consistency. I accept this now. You've never been strayed by fads or corrupted by money from the larger studios. You're no martyr, either. You take the money you need to take, but never so much that it compromises you in any way. And this is what we're left with. This is the result. Something of power and wonder. You don't shoot films to consciously create beauty, but somehow it is found. You work with two of the most promising new actors yet there are no vanity shots. Instead, you allow them the space to work in their surroundings, your camera no more than your eye, turning over rocks to find diamonds. I couldn't breathe by the end of it, maestro. I've been carrying the essence of Maxwell's book with me for years without realising it, I said. The stillness and sadness. Our capacity for love, and the failures that come from not speaking up. It's only when I reread it after my last film that the penny dropped and I realised that I had to visually interpret it. Well, in your usual quiet way, you've devastated me, he said. There's no question that I'll be living with this film for a long time, and for that, I'm happy. The declaration was sealed with a handshake and a kiss on both cheeks. It was for this that Gabi had worried, for each of the three had given no sign on leaving their private screening that afternoon, no more than half an hour after I had run the reels alone with the projectionist. I sweated buckets while you were off enjoying yourself, she said. In that two-hour running time, I lost several stone. Now everyone was sufficiently relaxed, the dinner still purposeful regarding the demands of the following days, but gently irreverent and free. By the fish course we had stopped talking of the schedule entirely, marvelling instead at the work coming from the kitchen: the miraculous comfort of the black risotto; the hare which tasted of the woods, in harmony with the fungi and red wine sauce that dressed it. Lorien whistled his surprise as each plate was brought, and then wolfed it down without a word. Tom was similarly speechless, his eyes taking it in, before regaining himself to ask a dozen questions about each dish's origin, ingredients and preparation. He was an epicurean in his make-up, remnants of a farm boyhood, and it was pleasing both to answer what I knew and to bow to my learned kitchen friends when I did not. My husband had found this restaurant many years before, left to his own devices at a previous festival, which I had insisted on dragging him to early in our relationship; wanting to show off, but at the same time frozen by the weight of the gesture. I deliberately kept myself busy when I didn't need to and gave him no time. Frustrated by my coldness, he considered leaving early on several occasions but never followed it through, knowing that I would thaw once I'd fully assimilated to the festival's inner rhythm and then return to him a functioning human being. Equally, he would never make me forget how selfish and isolating I had been. It was in the period long before we married when our outcome could have radically altered. If he'd left during that festival week, by his design it would've been over. In finding this restaurant deep in the city's working heart, in pulling me away from the festival's bubble, to

a place where my obsessions were unimportant, secondary
to both the food and the company sitting across from me, he
saved our relationship. Our foundations were created over
that meal, what was acceptable and what was not, the definition of what life meant to each other; put on the spot for
our interpretations of what constituted personal success and
living well. He forced out of me things I typically only gave
credence to on film, afraid of showing the same vulnerability
that had choked previous relationships. But he was not those
others; he was himself, thoughtful and willing to fight. A
space opened up that enabled the possibility of our marriage
to exist, making the restaurant itself more than just a gastro-
nomic home, but a place where family could be created from
ruins. Gabi and the publicist cried off dessert, a meeting with
a British distributor calling them back to the hotel. In leaving the three of us at table, a much-anticipated equilibrium
was restored; it showed in our effusive farewells and the
comfortable silence that settled between us afterwards.
Lorien, five years older than Tom, more strongly built and
better read, was slower to our tempo. Once reseated, he was
content to finish the plate before him, while Tom waved his
fork and enthused. When he glanced up into his younger
co-star's face, there was a look of pride and adoration,
undeniable and acknowledged by all. It's the pasta that blew
me away, Tom said. You think it's good in New York, and
then you taste this and it's like something from another
planet. Gabi took me to a place the other night, and the pasta
there blew my mind, but nothing on this scale. It's flour and

eggs, right? Just those two things, yet in different hands the results are so different. This was firm, yet it was like eating silk. How can I say it right? It . . yielded in my mouth, maestro. The firmness gave way to the soft. Something like a dream. How do they do that? Wow, he mouthed silently, as if recognising the greater power in explaining without voice. Wow wow wow. If you think this is bad, you should see what he was like when I introduced him to sourdough up in the hills, joked Lorien. Damn near lost his mind. Flour and water, man, said Tom. The power of flour and water. How come we don't recognise how holy that can be in the right hands? There's enough people who do, trust me, said Lorien. When I was shooting in Jerusalem year before last, there's a flatbread that they have. This beaten-up dough that's rolled thin and then fried to a crisp in front of you, and then smashed, so that it looks like rags. Like, street food. They top it with an egg and have it for breakfast. Holiness in those hands right there. The paratha I tasted in India, the same thing. You'd see people fall into a daze over it, but that may have been the endorphins from the amount of butter that goes into each one. You couldn't eat those every day and expect your arteries to keep going, that's for sure. Gandhi once said there are people in the world so hungry that God cannot appear to them except in the form of bread. Same rule applies here, right? It was Tom's turn now to look rapt, his eyes never leaving Lorien's face as he spoke. He was pliant, soaking up what Lorien had to give the way the still-warm pasta sucked-up the remains of the sauce. He'd known

nothing of bread's holy qualities and now he did. It was
lodged somewhere, filed, so that one day he could speak
with the same authority should he have the confidence to
do so, but most of all was he was in thrall to Lorien's knowledge and experience: the casualness with which it was
thrown out, and how generously it was shared. The history
of this generosity, a mixture of admiration and disbelief that
it could still be real, was plain in his face. I'm just a kid who
was thrown together with you for a movie that wrapped
months ago, he seemed to say. Why aren't you bored of me
yet, with my endless questions and tagging along? They were
inseparable during the shoot and remained so now. It was
hard to think of a situation which would break that. Once
flour and water bond, its tensile strength cannot be underestimated, I said. In ancient civilisations they daubed houses
with it, plastering their rooms when other materials couldn't
be found. Man, you guys know everything, Tom complained with a laugh. I could give you some line about how
my mom made bread every other day on the farm, but they
grow corn and potatoes, with a few chickens on the side. We
bought our sliced bread from the store same as everyone else.
Humdrum folks. Lorien poked him gently on the shoulder
as if to hush the noise. There's nothing humdrum about you,
Tom, he said, with such affection I suddenly felt like an
intruder and had to look away. Only in my peripheral vision
did I see Tom accept this with a barely shifting nod of his
head. We sent the cars away, deciding to walk back to the
hotel. The sky was clear, the ground cold; the greatest chill

felt against the backs of our legs and on our faces. We would've walked whatever the weather, acknowledging that we didn't want the evening to end. In many ways it felt like we had only been talking for five minutes. Does anyone know where we're going? asked Lorien, saying what he thought needed to be said, but with enough nonchalance in his tone to suggest his readiness to wander. We have the GPS on our phones and a collective memory, I said. That's more than enough to cobble a route together. But no route was planned. We walked and carried on walking. I took comfort in the trio of shadows falling behind us, a unit whose allegiance was unquestioned. During the making of the film I had taken them on similar walks, a habit fostered in the pre-production weeks before shooting began, and then sporadically when the photography allowed. I wanted them to feel the fabric of their location through their footsteps; how in walking through a town at night, you learned of its true nature, its rhythms and idiosyncrasies. It was more than the passing voyeurism as people dressed or undressed through windows yet to be drawn, or in the silence of the main thoroughfares, with its occasional disturbance of passing cars. The warmth of the silence enveloping you as you walked, aware of your breath and those of your companions; how your steps would fall into line at times, each of us consciously making it so, both jokingly and to physically demonstrate that we were attuned. We were not drunk on the shoot, but we were now, happily so. Why didn't you want to see the film before tomorrow? I asked. I'm intrigued.

You know why, said Lorien, or at least you should know. We saw the rough cut and went crazy for it, said Tom. Our agents saw the rough cut and they were the same. For now that's enough. Do you know how many films I make where I don't get to see anything? said Lorien. You work and work and work. Either there's no time to spend in screening rooms or you're not in town for it. I saw a movie I had a small part in two years ago only the other day on an airplane. This is how low down on the food chain we can be. And never mind me, said Tom. I'm just starting out. Who gives a fuck about my opinion? But I don't work that way, I said, and I've always tried to make you aware of it. When I offered you a screening in the edit suite before we sent the print for its final grading, it wasn't an empty gesture. We understand that, maestro, said Lorien, and we're grateful. If another director had asked me the same I would've bitten his hand off. Same, said Tom, but we made a pact on the flight home. Making this film has been unlike any other experience, Lorien explained. We know it and you know it. I remember saying to Tom, Man, I've trusted this guy like I've never trusted anyone in my life. Something of that belief has to be carried through in the completion of the film. If we don't allow him to cut the film the way it needs to be done, then we haven't done our jobs right. Do you see, maestro, there was no resistance because we trusted you so implicitly. Our performances couldn't have happened without it. If we can trust him in those circumstances, I said to Tom, we can trust him to get the edit right. We can turn up to opening night without fear because he loved and respected us, and wouldn't let us down. Oh, and there was a five-grand wager on it, said Tom, laughing, his pitch higher from the wine. First person to cave had to hand over the cash. What's this statue we're passing, by the way? Does it have any significance? They all have significance, I said. There's a famous saint that comes from here, and this is a statue to celebrate her origins. We paused to take in the iron cast atop a tall plinth, of a young girl crouching on the ground to feed three pigeons, barefoot and dressed in rags. When cities were countries in themselves, this girl travelled without favour to feed the poor and was made a martyr because of it. My head was swimming with the history of saints, because if I responded to the story of their bet, and beyond that, their implicit trust in me, filial and unconditional, I would have become undone. Every city has its saint, isn't that right? asked Tom, wanting to share what he'd learned. Do you remember the saint's statue near the town square when we were shooting? he said. That was the war memorial, contradicted Lorien, or *a* war memorial, at least. I'm not talking about that one, Tom said, but the one in the arches behind the plaza. By the public water fountain. The nun. She threw herself from the convent roof rather than surrender to occupying forces. So it *is* a war memorial, said Lorien. You're getting your dedications mixed up. No, Tom's right, I said. She had many visions that enabled her bravery. They made her into a saint. Ha! Tom punched the air, victorious. I'm surprised that you know that story, I said, it's fairly obscure. You lump us in with Italians for two months, and they tell you a few stories, he said. That's how it goes, maestro. Curious mind, me. You should come back and look at this statue, called Lorien. Something about it seems to have changed. We turned, not realising how far we had walked on ahead. Lorien, standing by the statue, his back to us. It must be some kind of miracle, he said, quite seriously. We could not detect the change at that distance through the darkness and retraced our steps, Tom running ahead of me, as eager for Lorien to not be alone as to discover the nature of the transformation. Again, I took note of the unspoken that was shared between them, how their need to be together was far stronger than a union of three. It had to be accepted over the course of the festival, celebrated and mourned. The crouching saint was now wearing a scarf covering her head, folded into a triangle and tied under her chin, making her posture as one of the people even more pronounced. My scarf! Tom tapped his empty jacket pocket as if the evidence of touch was greater than sight. You pick-pocketed me! Lorien laughed. It fell from your pocket just now. You were getting too serious on the saints, man. The temptation was too much. Great, said Tom, his eyes fixed to the top of the statue, lips pinched with distaste. And now it's going to be stained with bird crap. Nice job. You're mad at me? Lorien asked. I thought it would raise a laugh, is all. Easy for you to dismiss this stuff as junk, said Tom, his voice continuing to lift. You're used to these trophies. I'm not. Do you think we have Gucci where I come from? He was moving away from Lorien in his anger, standing equidistant between us now as the confusion on his face became clear. The conflict lay in the joy of the prank itself running parallel to the burn that something he deemed precious was seen as easy pickings. If Lorien could be dismissive of a scarf he'd only gifted the day before, in what other aspects of his life was he that throwaway? What you're saying is that I messed up, said Lorien, who held up his hands. I'm sorry, dude. Mean it. What I'm saying is to respect the garment, said Tom. He smiled now, conscious of his earnestness, but still holding Lorien's gaze as if to make himself clear. For all the shared ease, and the belief that he had found his people, he was still never far from self-loathing. It was this emotional openness that made him such an intuitive actor, but the difficulty of living with that suddenly seemed greater than my self-inflicted woes. Tom walked up to Lorien and softly head-butted him in the chest. You're an idiot, you know that? As long as I'm your idiot, said Lorien, quieter now, as he held him by the shoulder. They stood quietly for a moment before Tom shook himself free, roused into action. Now I'm going to have to climb up there to get it! Don't just stand there laughing, give me a leg-up. How the hell did you get it up there in the first place? We didn't hear a thing. Of course you didn't hear a thing, you were getting dreamy about your saints, said Lorien. You can shut up about that now, laughed Tom. Come on, help me. Get over here, maestro! We need a hand. Lorien might have put it up there, but he'll kill me if I leave it. You bet, laughed Lorien, do you know much that small piece of fabric set me back? Voyeurism worked both ways; the freedom we felt in walking the streets must have also been conferred on those who may have watched from their windows: our protracted efforts to push Tom up on to the plinth, and in retrieving the scarf, the delicacy of lowering him down. Lorien had the height advantage, no more than several inches, but it impacted on his agility and strength. He showed no signs of exertion, while Tom was red-faced and puffed out. It's the pasta slowing me down, he complained. That fucking pasta. Hysteria rang as we walked onwards. I took a picture before I called you, said Lorien. I'll send it to both of you later. Don't put it on any social media in case I'm crucified for disrespecting a saint. Just between us. I had my own reasons for shame. My husband had proposed to me beside that statue walking home from the restaurant a year after he had first taken me there. Three years later I had disrespected the same monument by spitting on it after a phone argument with him, wanting to debase the happier memory; the acid from my mouth reducing it to rubble. I could not share this with the boys for fear of what they would think of me; indeed, I had never shared it with my husband, instead apologising for my failings the moment I returned to the hotel. I'd been recovering from a chest cold, and remember the thick foaminess of my phlegm as it ran down the side of the plinth; the deepest expression of hatred I could muster for a man I thought misunderstood me. (On the contrary, he understood me too well and would not tolerate my distracted bullshit, hence the argument.) I was not a monster, but film could make a gargoyle of me, felt by those who were closest, and it was indiscriminate: in the time before my husband I would routinely attack myself for the failure that I was. The statue was and remained a turning point. From then I worked hard to quell further ugliness, and if anything, further healing came from Lorien's joke, associating that street with happier memories again; the scarf breaking a previously dour spell. The unknown ways in which memory guides your body cannot be divined: from a pathway to the statue, and now bypassing the main road to follow the railway tracks, and the disused factories which ran alongside. It was the first time that evening that I'd thought of Cosima and my failure to text her earlier when she'd contacted me again. If the offer to see the film is still open, I'd be delighted to see it, she said. Or if you need to go walking again. Another failure. But there were still other ways to honour her. There's something I want to show you, I said. Something I discovered today. If it's anything to do with alcohol I'm in, maestro, said Lorien. A nightcap some-where incredible would hit the spot. Afterwards, I said. This will be a worthwhile detour, I promise you. Guided by the factory skyline, we negotiated the maze of streets until the way became familiar to me. In all the photographs taken that afternoon I'd neglected to record either the name of the street or the front of the apartment building itself. Darkness slowed our navigation, leading to a number of dead ends which hampered the boys' enthusiasm. You know what would hit the spot right now? asked Lorien drily. The warmth of the hotel bar, with a cocktail waiter lining them up. I don't think I'm capable of drinking any more, said Tom. The dessert wine we had with that curd tart nearly finished me off. I'm wondering if I'll ever reach an age where I can get through a grown-up five-course meal without being a lightweight. That's why you're so lucky to have found me, said Lorien. I don't think there's anything I'll ever be able to teach you about acting – you have far too much talent for that. But drinking. That's something I can help you with. Don't ruin me, Tom laughed, I can't lose these boyish good looks. If I had my way you'd stay like that for ever, said Lorien under his breath with a seriousness that made the three of us instantly separate to avoid the gravity of those words. We resorted to acting, examining various shadows and cobbles, and pretending that nothing had been said. We walked gloomily along the factory road, the romance of both my earlier walk with Cosima and the dinner itself lost. For the first time Lorien looked uncomfortable and began to talk about calling the car, to take them to another part of town at least, if not to the hotel. I think this walk is getting a little too real, he said. I thought we were looking for treasure rather than deprivation, at this time of night, especially. This isn't the same as those midnight walks we took on set, maestro. That beautiful little Italian town where nothing happens. In cities the atmosphere changes from street to street. It changed for us twenty minutes ago when we started walking along the tracks. Don't you feel it? I feel too many things, I wanted to say. I

feel the weight of this city's history and my own, loaded on
my back. I feel desire, sadness and regret for the time that's
left to us. You two are too young to appreciate how fragile
time is. The reason I make films is because I never want the
present to be over, pushed by the impossible wish to extend
the moment. We walk along this shitty street, but it belongs
to just the three of us. It's cold and we walk through darkness, yet still I want to prolong the moment, because as soon
as we reach the hotel that moment ends. I make films
because as much as I obsess over the final moment, its composition and tone, what it must deliver structurally and
emotionally, I wish to run from it. Months of planning and
still I want to run. My films, races all. My heart was beating
fast now, both from the memory of those races and the
increased pace of our walk. It felt as though my thoughts
were amplified; how everything that rushed through me had
to show on my face, discernible through the darkness. But
they were walking slightly ahead, and if they picked up on
the descent of my humour, they did not comment on it. My
pace was working to keep up with theirs, as they walked
towards the sounds of the main road. It's art I'm taking you
to, I said, or at least trying to. It's not just his work that's
incredible, but his story also. Hidden, private art. A lost
graffiti artist from the eighties. I only found out about him
this afternoon. At that they stopped and turned around, their
curiosity greater than their discomfort. The transparency of
actors! For all their honesty, they came back because they
knew there might be a story there, and stories were their

lifeblood. I was not among those of my contemporaries who dismissively viewed actors as something akin to vampires: gorging on their collaborators until they were reduced to husks, and then moving on to the next. How only vampires could be actors because they were precisely ruled by their emptiness, only coming to life through the stories of others. I was not of that belief, understanding that it was the biography of the actor that gave the role its essence; that in many ways I was shooting the life of the characters as well as the biography of the actors in making the film. But running alongside that tenet, I still saw the hunger in Lorien's eyes. If I had a camera to hand, I would have pulled focus on his face and kept it there. I'm not a fan of tight close-ups, my work marked by the use of a single lens, the frame itself mostly in mid or wide shot to best observe the actors' movement. If there are five people sitting at a table, I want to see the full range of responses of those five people as the action is being played out; the involuntary tap of a foot against a chair leg being as important as their facial expressions, their tones and silences. But every ounce of Lorien's energy was fixed on his eyes, and it felt sinful not to capture it. I met a woman this afternoon, and she took me to this place, I said. This incredible graffiti mural in the garden of an apartment block. Hardly anyone gets access to the place, but it's something you should see. We're going to bust into an apartment block at midnight? asked Lorien. This all sounds great, but people who don't know you will think it's kind of crazy. Art drives you to do crazy things, said Tom. Do you know of any other director who'd take you on an art hunt in a broken-down part of the city in the middle of the night, just because we needed to see it? Lorien blinked at him and nodded. This had nothing to do with the film we had just made, but conversely, it had everything to do with it. I continued to ask for trust when they had no need to give it. But here we were. Lorien gripped my shoulder, the squeeze his affirmation that he was on board, had always been on board, even when he was reticent to show it. Lead the way, maestro, he said. As the outline of the factories became again familiar to me, my confidence returned. He came from this area, I said. His mother worked in this glove factory here. He met his future girlfriend in the one alongside. Tom's face was turned towards the building fronts, their scale monolithic, and their depths unknown through the darkness. We had factories in my home town, he said, on the outskirts. A place that made umbrellas, and another that printed baseball cards you used to find in packets of candy. They closed down before I was born, I think when my dad was a kid, as far back as that. Only they never did anything with the buildings. They were never sold, and no one tried to take them over. They were abandoned, left to fall to pieces. It's strange, because I feel comfortable here. The smell's the same. Ghosts. Grease. If I touch my hand on this wall and close my eyes, I'm home, or at least, a short ride from it. If Lorien echoed Tom's train of thought by touching the wall also, there would have been magic, but he was not given to sentiment over place. He came from the city and carried with him metropolitan assumptions and privileges. That was not to say that he was insensitive to the wonder of shooting a film on a mountainside, or the pace of village life; he found a way to make it harmonious with his world view. In many ways he took the most from his surroundings and used it in his work, only once that work was done it did not move him in the same way. Like Tom, he heard the ghosts from the factory, but unlike him, he did not respond to their call, standing apace; the look on his face, of astonishment and tenderness, related only to Tom, and in learning something new about him; more wonderment, from over eight months of wonders. All I hear are people bitching about overtime, he joked, and then said quite seriously, and of people ruining their hands. I'm thinking of the transformations that take place. How a young boy starting in a job like that loses his softness over time. Starting with the hands. How callused, battered, they must be by the end. He was looking at Tom's hand with its palm flat on the factory wall. His skin was so pale it shone luminously through the grey-black light. Waiting for Tom to leave his dreaming, for him to make eye contact, he took his hand and kissed it. Imagine this hand getting calluses, he said, his career would be over! What roles would there be left to play? Laughing again now, recognising his responsibility as the older brother to pull everyone out of the mire. Dressed up as an ape or shooting films down coal mines. We can't let that happen to this baby. You're a dick sometimes, said Tom, killing my poetry with your poetry. I'm teaching you about one-upmanship, declared

Lorien. You need to learn it if you want to spend time around actors. If you're willing to blend into the background they'll eat you alive. We had energy now, and in reaching the apartment block I was in high spirits, eager to find a way into the garden. If they saw what I saw they would understand something of my transformative afternoon. There was still something in its essence that I didn't wish to share, something yet to be processed that would only come through reflection, maybe writing or a series of photographs. What passed between Cosima and me wasn't important to them. Only the art mattered, and this they needed to see. I know we've been saying that it's midnight for ages now, but it is officially midnight, said Lorien. There are no lights on in this building, so what's your plan? The building's empty, I said. It's been empty for the last two years. You've brought us all the way here to stand outside an empty building? said Lorien. Was this really the best time? He said it was significant, said Tom, you can see it's important to him. What else would we be doing? Surrounded by hangers-on in the hotel bar? There's some pretty things hanging around in that hotel bar, said Lorien. You haven't noticed because you've been too busy working. If a frost passed between them, I did not see it, too consumed with the riddle of the locked door. There's a caretaker in the basement, I said eventually. It's just a question of finding the right doorbell to ring. Maestro, we can't rouse people from their beds at this hour, said Tom. I really want to see this art, but people will think we're nuts. Especially since there's an easier time to see it. You've seen the schedule, I said, we're prisoners of the hotel for most of tomorrow and the day after that. I was compelled by the urgency of the moment. I still can't explain why, but madness of a kind gripped me. If I could have found a wall to climb, I would have pushed myself up. If there was loose masonry around the street I would have picked the nearest rock and smashed one of the glass door panels to gain entry. Different aspects of Cosima's story were becoming important to me, none more so than the image of the boy artist working alone at night, his shadow alternately cast over the apartment block and the wall itself as the moon rose. If we could stand in the garden under a similar moon glow, I felt that we would see him and understand how he worked, answering all my questions about the mural's joins. I'd underestimated the magnetism of the piece, how it would draw me back. When I'd left the building with Cosima that afternoon, I was certain I would never return, but its claim on my heart and my feet were undeniable, driving me forward. Both of you got up on that plinth without too much difficulty, I said. Could you get over a wall if we needed to? Maestro, I like seeing the mischief in your face, but something tells me that illegal entry isn't the right way to go, said Lorien. If there's truly something great to see, we can arrange it in the morning. What's the use of having these producers and fixers hanging around if we can't make them sweat a little and make a few things happen? Rabbits out of hats. You chicken now? asked Tom. I had this mental picture of you heroically scaling walls in your sleep. That's the chronic untruth about movies, said Lorien. Everything you see is a lie. Almost everything, said Tom shyly. Yes, almost, said Lorien. What interrupted us was a growing light, not from the building's depths, but outside: the lights from an SUV leaving the main road and approaching the apartment block. You called them, I said to Lorien, the despair in my voice plain and seeming to age me as it echoed above the car's gradual roar. This part of the programme's a bust, maestro, he said. Let's get somewhere warmer while we figure out what to do. And by warmer, I mean somewhere with alcohol. How far's the hotel? asked Tom. Fifteen minutes, if that, said Lorien. This city's a maze, but in terms of its footprint it doesn't stretch very far. In less than twenty minutes we can have a last round of booze inside us, and then retire to dreams about art unseen. In the car I felt off balance and foolish, overwhelmingly aware of being the architect of a failed experiment. There was no shame in failure, only in not trying, but the abrupt end to the evening left me numbed and vulnerable. I'd wanted to return to the hotel elated, the boys wide-eyed and excited by the mural and the story behind it. I needed to feel that I was still an essential part of their education, that without me the hidden stories that could potentially change them would be lost; to be seen as a diviner of secrets and stories; that my ability to surprise and educate was constant. I wanted to be invaluable to them, the way I felt my own family to be. Instead, I had become over-excited and needed to be reasoned with, a confused parent who wasn't making any sense. For the first time I saw myself through their eyes, and my fallibility was inescapable. On set I was king; outside a locked apartment block, drunk, less so. Sooner or later even the most devout turn against their gods, and I had engineered a schism of my own making; my spontaneity backfiring, with only sore feet and reddened noses to show for it. I was also aware now that the joy of spending time in each other's company had its limit, the two of them talking quietly on the back seat, as I closed my eyes in the front next to the driver. I was jealous? Tired? A little of both. Sad? Yes. Out of kilter, also; self-conscious and unsure how to reassert myself. How to come between a couple who were ready to be alone, who were in love and did not realise its depths? I had made a film about two young men in denial of their true feelings, and now it was being played out in the back of the SUV. They were both looking out of the window on Lorien's side, as he pointed out a store that interested him, not sitting tightly, but near enough for their knees to touch. They were tactile with each other, always had been, from the demands of the film and the time they'd shared. I'd worked with the most expressive actors who were cold fish off camera, not wanting to be touched or seen. What Lorien and Tom shared was rooted in joy and the discovery of brotherhood. The rest was private and would remain that way. I wanted to see the film in their faces and through their body language, as if by trans-posing what had been shot on to a real-life canvas, it further immortalised the truth we had achieved. But which was the truth – mine or theirs? I was ready to argue the case all night.

I knew I would struggle to sleep now the debate was clear in my mind. Was the film more important than the life that came afterwards? Which would be remembered, and where lay the true art – in something meticulously scripted, or in a space that flourished off the page? Will you hang around for a nightcap? asked Lorien. I've just found out that this boy here has never had a Brandy Alexander, which is something we need to rectify asap. Save me from this alcohol-fixated thug, laughed Tom, batting Lorien away in a mock wrestle. The purity of his happiness nearly broke my heart. He'd pushed himself on screen, given everything, but here was the one nugget he'd managed to save for himself. I need to go upstairs and call my husband, I said. We haven't spoken properly all day. As you know, he writes when our kid's asleep, so he should still be up. Give him our love, said Tom, and Sleeping Beauty, too. Our. In the space of the car journey something confirmed. Lorien shifted in his seat on hearing it, but only closer to Tom. Our journey. Our secret. See you bright and early, he said. One brandy and we'll be out like lights. It does that to you. I was hugged and thanked for dinner, sincerity in their eyes and hold. It seemed to negate the worst of the wild goose chase. All they would remember was the horseplay around the statue and the symmetry of their walk, for only through darkness and the absence of prying eyes could they reveal themselves. I'll send you the photographs of the mural when I'm back in my room, I said, but they were already away, disappearing through the lobby and the bar that lay beyond. The end of the night was also the start, one to which I did not belong. In my room I called my husband and told him about the interview and the dinner. I told him about the projectionist who hugged me, and how I felt the warmth of that even now. You're too tired, he said, I can hear it in your voice. You should be over the moon, even by your muted stand-ards, but I can't detect any of that. You just sound devastated. Is everything all right? I'm getting too old for this, I said. The rollercoaster of expectation. I've been juggling it all day. I used to feed off it, but now it makes me tired. This is noth-ing we haven't discussed before, he said. You're talking this way because you haven't had enough sleep. Make time for that. There's always time for that. But I can't sleep now, I said, my pitch rising, as if caught in a lie. I feel too wide awake. The spacing between your words tells me another story, he said. Also the wine in your voice. You'll sleep easy, because I'm telling you it's possible, and you've never had reason to doubt what I say. We talked of our boy and our plans for the next day, which balanced my mind somewhat. Our son had a football tournament he was looking forward to, and the pleasure it gave him, his incipient joy in running and scoring, being part of the team, acted as a salve. My husband always knew how to depressurise my invisible weight. Life was waiting for me at home, the trials and joys of living; the truth was there and not in this made-up world. I lay on the bed afterwards but sleep would not come. I could only think of Lorien and Tom in the hotel bar, and later, elsewhere. I texted them the photos of the mural as I'd promised, but they did not respond. I searched for the TV remote, thinking I would watch a movie, that there had to be at least one film in the library that could both speak to me and send me off. Watching movies was my other constant. If you did not watch countless films how could you know what your work was worth? The remote was on the desk, and in getting up to retrieve it I saw a package there also, with a note from Gabi. It was the fulfilment of a request I'd made that afternoon: to source copies of Cosima's books. I had forgotten about her work, but now it was here in my hands.

4.

Gabi had been unable to find the non-fiction but had produced the novel and a small book of short stories. There were two copies of the stories, one in French and one in Italian, both hardcovers. The novel, a paperback, was in Italian only. The stories were called *Model, Upstairs*, the novel, *Far From the Hurting Kind*, both published over twenty-five years ago. I thought of Cosima in her youth, writing these books, and of my youth also, the intense period when I made my first three films. She'd been writing through the time of her romance and the period of their prolific creativity. This is what she'd neglected to mention when she spoke of those hours spent in his mother's apartment: the cherished silence in which they worked together. She'd mentioned portraits, but were these portraits of her as she wrote? Questions I wanted to immediately ask, but I shied away from my phone. I knew that I would not sleep until I had read one of the books in its entirety. The life of the stories drew me, her first published work, but instinctively I reached for the novel, because what she had not told me had to be contained there. Gabi had the foresight to leave me an Italian dictionary, which I appreciated. My Italian was not rudimentary – indeed, I thought myself fluent having shot several films here – but I was tired and aware of the effort required of me. My husband was right, I needed to sleep for tomorrow was a long day, but there was no chance of that with Cosima's words on my nightstand. I was hoping to hear her voice through reading. I wanted the literary equivalent of the dry tone and the raised eyebrow; to draw the same harmonious conclusion that I had this afternoon. The novel was about a young girl living through grief. Her boyfriend dies by his own hand in a new city, and she moves there after the funeral, tracing his footsteps through the school he'd enrolled in and taking an apartment below the one he'd rented. She drinks espresso in the bar he'd visit each morning, and washes her clothes in the laundromat behind the market, as he'd described in his letters. As she tries to sleep each night, she hears the new tenant above walking around, a young man of similar age, and imagines that it is him: walking from the sofa to the fridge to grab another beer, smoking a last cigarette on the balcony before bed, the pummel of the mattress springs as he entertains a woman. She leaves her sweetheart's favourite pasta dish anonymously on his doorstep, and when that is accepted, follows with a further dish, a cassette of a band they followed, then a book of poems, and a Barbara Kruger print she once bought for

him at a museum shop, until one day she finds a note taped
to his door: Please stop leaving me gifts whoever you are.
She hides in her apartment unsure what to do. The gift-
giving has given purpose to her days, in a way that the
college course has not, for there she feels stifled and afraid
to express herself through drawing. She starts to post letters
through his door, brief lines closer to notes; the daily mis-
sives you leave the object of your affection: *have a great day,
your sandwich is on the top shelf in the fridge, don't forget to call the
plumber, I love you, I miss you, see you tonight.* All that can no
longer be said, scribbled and posted through his door when
he leaves for work. There's a month of happiness drawn from
this note-taking, but the neighbour's patience does not last.
She is almost caught one morning when he doubles back to
discover the postman's identity. It is only her quick thinking
in setting off the fire alarm which stops her from being
revealed. The next day the letterbox is sealed shut. She still
communicates the only way she can, by writing. His mother
returned her letters to him after his death, and she pulls lines
from each one as if to test him. *What was the number of the
bus I rode when the driver took a detour because a woman on board
was having a baby? Where were you the night you wrote that first
postcard about wanting to hurt yourself?* She channels her
unvoiced anger through her pen, fuelled by his silence.
When the door is changed, no longer allowing her to slide
paper underneath, she tapes them to his doorbell. *Did you
forget that you had commitments?* she writes. *What happened to
saving for our wedding and finishing your college course so that you*

*could teach art? Where do you get off being so selfish? Leaving me
to be blamed by your mother. Where were you when she hammered
at my door in the middle of the night? Hurling every insult and
putting me under every curse she could remember. May you never
find happiness. May you rot under a stone. The girl with no obligations, who can take a loving son from under his mother's nose and
reduce him to nothing. Who built up his confidence without checking
the foundations. May you know this pain tearing at my insides.
May you lose a child in even more horrible ways, and may you be
left alone to deal with it. A day later she came and clung to me
because we were all the other had, but we needed you here for your
presence naturally united us; both of the same mind in our worship
of you. Where were you? Why did you leave?* The girl realises
that she has reached a dead end. Her course finishes with a
certificate and a commendation, but she is unable to register
either the quality of her work or the praise of her talent. All
she sees is another way to express her pain. The neighbour
still lives above, but the notes cease, understanding now in
each footstep that he is not him, cannot be, will never be. It
would be easy to look for flaws, his haircut and bad diet (she
doesn't go to the floor of his apartment any longer, but still
looks through his trash). She recognises that in wanting to
criticise the man, she is, in her stumbling way, getting well.
But ultimately, when the course ends, she knows that a
turning must occur. She could stay in the apartment for
years, clinging on to this slow measure of healing, but as she
clears her studio space at the art school, she feels the weight
of her collected work in her arms, and finds the appetite for

something greater. The value of the year has accumulated without her realising. The artwork feels like a peeled scab in her hands, its ugliness and purpose necessary. Under this, her skin is renewed. She returns to her home town and rents an apartment in an unfamiliar district, away from his mother and direct memories of him. She will draw those streets when she is ready. In time she will return to the same cobbles and cast them in bronze. She'll create large paintings of the notes posted on the doppelgänger's door. She'll build an installation of apartment doors whose bells ring incessantly. She'll embroider a blanket with all the insults she was ever called by men, but work that is solely created on her terms and under her eye. The scale of the work petrifies her, but she knows that this is what she must to do to stay alive; that in mourning all the qualities that made him good, she neglected to understand that she was good too. I read the book in one sitting, pushing through my misunderstanding of the language in places, for she wrote all the speech in a local dialect, the prose itself peppered with colloquialisms which brought the agonies of the book to life. I felt exhilarated and bruised, my face wet with tears, yet bursting with optimism for the woman's reckoning and outlook for the future. It was a story that needed to be filmed – had to be filmed. Of that there was no question. All this came from Cosima's hand. The hand I had shaken, and held as she lit a cigarette in the wind. I would have touched that hand differently had I known. I would've bowed before it. The gesture sounds overblown but I was floored by the novel, its depth and honesty; its unvarnished portrait of grief, the ugliness of the righteous, and still through that, scant traces of dry humour: a note the man posts up on his apartment door after the second dish is left to inform the sender that he is allergic to onions. I laughed loudly over the onions, though I started crying again shortly afterwards. The unspoken decision, a collective one, regarding the art that is remembered and that which is left to fade is hard to tally, when the book I was holding was so transcendent, it seemed to glow in my palm. After my first three films, I had the luxury of knowing that my work would be remembered. I felt uncertainty in the films I made after that, yes, pushing myself to improve: to be a better writer, to understand the camera in ways that I hadn't previously, to trust my eye and my instinct, and to gather people around me who could support and challenge that. I rested on nothing but the drive to keep creating more work, not because I was showboating or capitalising on any perceived popularity, but because I had an inherent need to understand the world, and that could only happen with a camera in my hand. Nothing about making my films had been easy. Each one was associated with scars I carried long afterwards, but I recognised that what Cosima had done was much harder, for she had simply created within a void, not knowing whether her work would be published, let alone recognised. She sat and wrote every day, with no idea of the outcome. The bravery of that made a mockery of my efforts, cosseted as I had become. It was still the middle of the night, but I needed to talk to her as soon as possible. If not her, I needed to speak to someone, my head swimming with the beauty of the story, cut to shreds emotionally, but lifted because of it. I've just finished *Far From the Hurting Kind*, I texted. I'm still crying over it. This was surely the feeling of typing words into the void, for she did not reply – why would she at this hour? If through this I felt a minuscule percentage of her perception, a victory for determination over the weight of pain, then I was still unworthy to stand in her shoes. My room phone rang. I can't sleep, said Tom. You can't either, otherwise you wouldn't have picked up so quickly. What are you doing? Reading, I said, where are you? In my room, he said. I've left Lorien sleeping. He was the one who came off worse from the Brandy Alexanders. You should try to rest for a few hours, I said. It'll show on your face in the morning. It'll show on yours, too, he said. I'm old, I replied. They don't care if I have bags under my eyes. I'm not on camera to be desired. That's your job. I'm still figuring out how much liquor I can take, he said. Same as I'm figuring out other things. How to get to know a person. Really know them without it taking something of yourself away. You'll work it out, I said. Possibly when you're more awake. Urgh, there's no way I can get to sleep, he said. At least not yet. I'm too wired. From the alcohol? I asked. No, just from being around you guys, he said. You know why. Tom could never sleep. Nights following a full day's shooting and he'd still be up, climbing the walls. This is new to me, I remember him saying. I'm finding it hard to believe that I'll get to a stage where I take all this for granted. That after a day of work on set I'll unwind with a bowl of pasta and have lights out by ten thirty. How do you switch off, maestro? What do you do when everyone's gone and you're alone in your room? I plan the next day's work, I'd said to him. I think about what I want to achieve over what is possible. I watch movies. Close my eyes. He came over a few times to watch movies. Lorien, also. It was the only way to get any peace from them. Tom relaxed on a sofa the way he wouldn't in bed. More often than not, he fell asleep during the first hour of the movie. Was it the company he needed or a space to be unafraid? Now I said, I'd ask you to come and watch a film but it's too late for that. We should both try to get some rest. I just wanted to hear your voice, he said. What struck me at dinner tonight was how much I missed your voice. The conversations. Every time we talk I learn something new. Those statues we were fooling over tonight. The art we almost saw. I don't get this with anyone else, besides Lorien. We can always talk, I said. Just because we're not making a movie doesn't mean we can't talk. You know where I am, where I live. Well, that's the funny thing, he said. I had four weeks after we wrapped my last movie where I was twiddling my thumbs, and LA's not the place to be when you want to escape from your own noise. It's hell, I said, not wanting to tell him that the noise would always be there no matter which city you ran to. It was finding another person to shut out the noise that was the trick. A person who could stop you from running. Tom said, They were showing

Rome, Open City at one of the local movie houses, and I went to see it one afternoon, with your commentary running through my head from when you screened it at your place. Man, I missed that commentary so bad, I thought I was going to jump on a plane and get to your house. Just so we could sit in your living room and have conversations. I bought a new soccer ball for the kid. Imagined having a kick-around in your backyard. What stopped you? I asked. Auditions, he laughed. The demands of my ego over what I actually need. He got the soccer ball, right? It's his new favourite, I said. Never stops playing with it. Good, he said. I'm pleased. Cocteau once wrote, Imitate, and what is personal will eventually come despite yourself, I said. He was talking about filmmaking, but it applies to life outside of that too, don't you think? This is the conversation I'm talking about, said Tom. What I need in my life. I was too scared to jump on a plane. Rejection, whatever. A look on your face that said you're puzzled or disappointed in me. I could never be disappointed in you, I said, not when you're being yourself. You flatter me, he said. I'm just a kid who got lucky on a couple of films. That's still how I see myself, I said, on a good day. This is what I longed for, he said, you telling me about Cocteau. Giving me confidence. The film's finished so you have no obligation towards me, yet you're still in my corner. Why? This is how I live, I said. I don't know any other way. Tom said, Now I'm going to have to look up the Cocteau dude. Do you have any idea how uneducated I am? I go on sets sometimes and feel like the thickest person there.

Not with our film, though. Too many late-night conversations to school me. This is what makes us family, I said, the ability to call me in the middle of the night. If you stop doing that, we've got problems. Tom laughed. I promise to always rouse your household at three a.m. Good boy, I said, go and close your eyes. I'll see you at breakfast. You sleep when your heart is full. He would sleep, I would sleep, Lorien would sleep. My husband and child. As for Cosima, I didn't know, but could not worry about that now; the phone call capping the day so perfectly, I wanted to sing. Finally I undressed and pulled down the bed covers. I could sleep without thought, for all my thinking was done. For Tom, too, I hoped. I stopped fighting, and submitted.

5.

Cosima texted me at five thirty. I had slept deeply, but still responded to the first trill of my phone, as if my subconscious knew that I would wait for her. She wrote, How did you find those books?! I thought they were buried! It's time for them to be exhumed, I wrote back. Can we meet today? Thank you for that, she said. They feel like books from another era, so I've long been uncertain of their validity. To my life or anyone else's. But we can meet? I persisted. I don't have much time today, but there are so many questions. This is very unexpected, maestro, she said. I don't know if I'm capable of answering your questions. I'm unsure I can find the girl who wrote it because she's buried too, but I can try. When? I asked. I'm free now, if you like, she replied. It's too early in the morning for me to lie, so at least you'll know that I'll answer your questions as honestly as I can. I got dressed and walked to the Duomo where she was waiting on the steps. I thought you'd be lighting a candle, I joked. I

stopped doing that a long time ago, she said. Once I'd written the book I had no need for candles. But she had the look
of someone caught, and I knew if I stepped closer to her I
would smell a match's sulphur on her coat and around her
face. It was the first time she had lied, possibly shaken that
I had read the book, but still curious for my thoughts on it.
The tyranny of a creative ego: the willingness to make
yourself vulnerable to praise, even if it destroys you afterwards. Can we go inside, I asked, just for a minute so I can
remind myself of the place? She scrunched her face in mock
annoyance but nodded, not wishing her attendance there to
be noted or made a big thing of. The Duomo was the city's
landmark, its steps a casual meeting place, but the invitation
at six a.m. meant something else, an admission of ritual. It
piqued my interest as much as the book: how she spent her
days, how she lived. She wove her biography through all
aspects of her work in such a way that it was impossible not
to pry. Those who create art from what is private must
accept this, as I long since had. The question was, did she?
Mass was being said, so we could not wander as freely as I
wished, nor could we gaze at the frescoes without self-
consciousness. Admittance at this hour was for the devout
and I was not one of those. We both blessed ourselves with
holy water as we entered, however, complicit in ritual but
also accepting of it; tenets of our childhood which had never
left. There were close to fifty people in attendance that paid
us no mind, their eyes and ears trained on the priest, their
legs straining to run towards his feet for communion. They

crouched, bent and stood in succession like a team of preparing athletes. We walked under the arches towards the
nave, drawn by the candles' glow. I paid my tithe and lit
three candles, standing before them for a moment, allowing
the priest's tone to bless me, the closest I would allow holiness to touch my head. Once that was done, we left without
a word. The candles are for the film, I said presently. The
mumbo-jumbo in there no longer means anything to me,
but I'm not such a charlatan to turn down help from all
corners. Are you still in purgatory, maestro? She looked
ready to remind me of my earlier foolishness. No, I said. I've
ventured out of there. I had some praise from an unexpected
source yesterday, which put my nerves into perspective. She
laughed. Yes, well, I can see how praise can do that to a
person. I wouldn't know personally. The eyebrow. We
walked through the church square and crossed a main road
that led to a narrow warren of streets; our kind of streets,
slowly coming to life at this hour: bakeries and cafes opening, the turning-over of car and scooter engines, and lights
being switched on in the apartments overhead. If you haven't
eaten we could get coffee and bread here, she said, gesturing
towards a bakery that stood on the corner. I know you
haven't got long, so I guess you can satisfy your curiosity
over a couple of espressos. You could give me an entire day
and I would still have questions, I said, but let's try. The
bakery was tiny, but had a small table outside, which we
commandeered: Cosima pulling the chairs just so, enabling
us to talk closely, while I bought coffee and two jam-filled

cornettos. We were both nervous in that moment, with the walk no longer able to distract us; each wary of opening or answering, and framing what would then follow. It took a cigarette each and a few swigs of coffee before either of us got our nerve up. I wasn't exaggerating, she said. Those books have disappeared, so the idea that you not only found them but read one overnight is bizarre to me. Welcome, but bizarre. I didn't even tell you my surname, but you still managed to track the books. Where did you find them? I have a co-producer, I said, who knows everything I don't know, and if she doesn't, she knows someone who does. She asked around. Ah! That's how it works, she said. And do you always get what you want? Not always, I said. I could bend the truth and say rarely, but that isn't the case. Whatever the outcome, my requests are taken seriously, put it that way. But why did you even look? she asked. What made you want to read them in the first place? I was interested, I said. I'm always in awe of writers, even those who erroneously believe that they're forgotten. It's a belief held by many, she said. Both of those books disappeared almost immediately after they were published. How they became physical objects at all now seems like a miracle to me. How old were you when the novel was published? I asked. Twenty-five, she said. The short stories were published a couple of years before that. I thought of my first film at twenty-four; the child I was, still saying childish things. She'd grasped in one book what it had taken me another decade to master. A man my mother cleaned for worked at a publishing house, she said, an accountant, but he was kind enough to show it to some people there. Someone has to look at what you're doing to see whether it has any value, or if you're mad, said my mother. After Bruno died, I wrote morning, noon and night, and the family were worried about me. Did they read the books? I asked. Afterwards, she said, and by then they probably wished I was mad. They were horrified by how candid the writing was. I'm going to ask you a question now, maestro, so that it feels a little less one-sided. Do you often follow strange women and read their books? Only when they have a story to tell, I said. There's more to it than that, of which you understand. After yesterday. If you didn't, we wouldn't be here. She nodded. I'm teasing you, maestro, because I'm trying to find a way to make myself comfortable. I only ever gave a handful of interviews when those books came out, and this is what I'd forgotten: how exposing it can be, and at six a.m., even more so. I understand completely if you want to stop, I said. I'm happy to finish the coffee and enjoy this pastry. If anything, you've taken me somewhere new, and that's good enough. She shook her head, indicating that she wanted to continue. If someone wanted to talk to you about your first film now, what would you say? she asked. Would you be flattered, or is it a memory you wish to bury? The films exist in the world, I said. More so now. You can search me on the internet and see them all. It's not like when we were young. We had to track down films from the great masters because they weren't easily accessible, and that search meant something. You waited for a cinema or university society to have a season, or you rented a video from the local store one at a time, or you saw photographic stills in an essay and had to imagine the rest, or you caught a rare screening on late-night TV. What we learned was piecemeal. We never had the full picture because at the time it wasn't available to us. If you made a bad film you could get away with it. You'd live with the embarrassment for a while, and after a year or two it would reliably disappear. That can't happen now, so you must own your failures or grudges or disappointments. Books remain hidden, she said. They don't have the glamour of movie stars and auteurs. This country is awash with forgotten stories, although that matters little to me. I'm not a romantic. Of course when you write something your desire is that it should be read, because your wish to be understood is boundless. It eats you up. What failure does is force you to reassess what's important. The need for a writer to be read is a basic one, but so is the accomplishment of finishing the book itself. I wrote those books because there was something inside I had to expel: anger, dreams and pretensions. They exist because they came from my hand. That's what I'm most proud of. Who gets to know or not know about it means less as time goes on. Does it make you happy that I've read it, or do you feel ambivalent? I asked. When you asked me how I'd feel if someone asked about my first film, I think I'd be happy because even though I know it's terrible I accept the impact that it had, and recognise that it still has significance to me. Do I want to be the twenty-four-year-old who made that film again?

Possibly. That's the weak spot, for nostalgia's an easy noose to slip into. Creative death if you linger there, but still it beguiles. You've just answered your own question, she laughed. What is it with men? Ask for your opinion, but then go on to tell you what to think! I hadn't marked you down as one of those! Are you annoyed? I asked. No, she said, I think it's funny. No matter which side you bat, the male ego is as strong as your heartbeat. This is why there are so few women making films. They don't want to be told what to do, and find their creative expression elsewhere. Do you know what I enjoy about writing, maestro? The hours of it, writing pages and pages with no deadline and destination. How it's only my opinion that counts. There's no negotiation or compromise. I have no one to keep happy. No egos to check. If that comes at the expense of recognition, I can live with that. If the books were published again, how would you feel? I asked. One of the many things I took away from reading it last night was how relevant they still are. How the writing was so strong, that they needed to be celebrated and seen. It's something I would have to learn to live with, she said, taken aback, her arms pushing the table away, as if wanting distance from both me and that reality. The idea of young women reading my book now would frighten me. Why? I asked. Because I would be judged, she said, by those thirty years younger who have grown up with different tools. We didn't have the tools. You're right in what you said. We did learn everything piecemeal, and not just the films. She stood up and jerked her head towards the door.

I'll get us another round of these because I'm feeling a little warmly towards you. Five minutes ago, I was ready to rip your head off. There was no aggression in her voice, only resignation, reflecting the inevitability of conversations past. I felt woolly headed and clumsy, without making it clear how much I admired her book and her spirit in the writing of it. I was saddened that we had started off so badly, when all I had wanted to do was give praise. When she returned several minutes later, the mood lifted. I realised just now that you wanted to ask me other things, she said. I'm not entirely sure how we got here. Me neither, I said. You're a wonderful writer and I worried that I hurt your feelings in asking the wrong questions. And in admitting that, there was a feeling at last that we now understood each other. She smiled in assent. You want to know whether the book is true, she said. It's probably the first thing you thought of. It was the first question any of them asked, if that makes it any easier for you. I don't want to pry, I said, but just because of what I learned yesterday ... You want to know whether there's any separation between the artist and the art, she said. I wouldn't answer the journalists who asked me at the time, even the ones I respected, because I feared being tripped up. That someone more knowledgeable would tell me that I simply wasn't grieving the right way, or more brutally, that another writer had explored the same territory, only more successfully. But the same question coming from you, maestro, an artist who knows something about these things, is one that I'm happy to answer. You honour me, I said. The novel is a series of blurred lines, she said, between what happened and my imagination, as novels should be, but the bulk of events, the ones that you must be thinking about, are real. My intention was not to write a novel on the rawness of grief but of its paralysis. When my boyfriend died, I felt suspended. Unable to think or breathe. Unable to close my eyes, and when I finally did, there'd be no impetus to open them again. I sat on his mother's couch and felt nothing, heard nothing. Half the apartment block were buzzing around those two tiny rooms, and it didn't register. I wasn't sure whether I was floating or if the shock had turned me invisible. He no longer existed, and by his act, nor did I. But that's not for now. What I wanted to show in the book was the paralysis of life afterwards. The zombie life, where you're still living, but barely. You might even accomplish a few things, maybe you get through college or do well in your job, but you're still underpinned by a void whose logic you can neither banish nor explain. So you went to art school? I asked. Not quite, she said. I went back to university. All I'd done was defer my final year to be with him, and now he was no longer here I wanted to get as far away as possible. Nine months to finish my literature degree. I'm still not sure how I made the decision, but an impulse must have originated to break me free temporarily, enabling enough energy to pack my things and go. Maybe it was a survival instinct, either that or a serious level of morbidity, for I knew that if I was alone in another city I could shut myself away with no one to check up on me. In the same way that addicts can be sneaky, so too are the bereaved. The university was far enough away that I knew my parents would be unable to reach me without effort. On the other hand, I was confident that I could get home safely should I be out of my depth. These weren't conscious thoughts. They only came to me afterwards. I was unable to move. To think. Yet my body found a way to pack my things and go. It was saving me from a breakdown, but at the time I couldn't define it. Our bodies are always capable of surprise, I said, as well as our hearts; who we run to or away from. I wanted to tell her of my experience working with actors, who saw immortalised on screen actions they had no memory of doing, either consumed or locked away from the character they played. I thought of Lorien being filmed as he dug up a field; how his effort and concentration went beyond the parameter of what the camera saw. There was no close-up, even though he was crying. He pitched and dug, clearing the soil with care, and then angrily, pushing the full force of his body with each thud and fling of the spade, as if challenging himself to create a hole deep enough to bury his emotion. Even now, it's a scene I can't watch without a tightening in my chest. Tom cried, too, when he saw it. But when Lorien looked at the playback afterwards, he was ignorant to the extent of his actions, not least the size of the grave. I was just digging, maestro, he said. Trying not to get out of breath. Trying to see past the mud. As for the rest, I don't know. The lesson from my daydream was clear. We have to worship our bodies for the job that they do, I said to Cosima. How we're protected without realising at times. It hasn't happened since, she laughed. I'm left to my own devices now. But you were looked after when it mattered, I said. That's the important part. Yes, you're right, maestro. I'd never thought about it in that way before. If I was mature enough to understand that at the time, I would've included it in the book. You think of it as juvenile now? I asked. The novel? I believe it to be the work of a young person of limited experience, yes, she said. We shouldn't pretend otherwise. That's not to say that I'm not proud of it. When the accountant from my first publisher died a few years ago, I sent the biggest flowers on behalf of my family. They were probably too vulgar for the funeral in retrospect but I wanted to demonstrate the depth of gratitude I owed him, and, by extension, accept the pride I had in those first two books. It brought back much I'd forgotten. Good things. She walked me back to the hotel, alerted by the growing traffic that our coffee had lasted longer than planned. There was a comfortable silence between us, an understanding reached, but also dissatisfaction that we had cut short a discussion that each of us wanted to expand upon. I could see in her eyes how much she wanted to speak, having finally found a space where it was safe to do so. When you are faced with someone who has had to fight for the freedom to work creatively, and you accept that you have given them the space to discuss and express their ideas when there has typically been only absence, you must be humble to your privilege. My space came from pushing myself to make one film after the next, how I could never sit still, for to do so would mean a closing of that space and the opportunities available to me. I was born with none of these things, nor had family who understood them. I too fought for a space that was mine. I worked in film not only because the camera felt like an extension of my hand, but because I enjoyed having a company around me; the inherent joy and frustration that came from collaborative effort. I was a coward in that regard, working best when I felt the presence of others around me, whether it was my husband and child moving through the house as I worked on my script, or in the production office, discussing plans with Gabi and my long-time editor Stjepan. After my first few films I took the forum for granted; there was always someone to speak to, lovers and colleagues I trusted enough to talk my rough ideas – and fears – through. Cosima spoke as a woman who had internalised those conversations, both from the necessity of protecting herself and from a failure to find her people. I'd been a visiting professor at a film school in Madrid for a number of years, and this is one of the first things I'd say to the students there. Find your people! Open yourself up until you find those you can trust, who believe in your talents and will both complement and challenge them. Be generous enough to do the same with others. Work on the films of those you love as well as projects of your own. Use everything you've internalised but don't let that limit you. You cannot make films if you're unable to speak or to accept the presence of other human beings. Without those things you're simply creating art installations, important in themselves, but they are not cinema, and that is what I'm here to teach you. I was jealous of the lives novelists lived but I knew that I was not a solitary creature. Novels were a different kind of cage, one where you willingly locked yourself in. Cosima had something of the captive in her, I thought; that same mixture of passion and restraint I'd seen in other novelists I'd worked with. No matter how open they were, I was always aware of their ability to shut themselves away, making the real world one to be studied and tolerated if not truly loved. Will you come and see the film tonight? I asked. There'll be plenty of people there, and we can have a chance to talk more afterwards. About the book? she asked. Aren't you bored of that yet? Absolutely not, I said. If anything, it seems to resonate more with me now than it did last night. Come to the screening. I might have some suggestions for you, but we can discuss that later. I realised as I was speaking that I wanted to adapt her novel for my next film; that I could not live with myself if I did not attempt it. For Cosima was right, I had been in purgatory, but not for the reasons she thought. My mind was a desert, scratching around for ideas for what could follow *The Folded Leaf.* Previously I had two or three films mapped out at one time, so that my trajectory was known. I was spared the dreaded free fall as each film wrapped because I was mostly certain of what was coming next. It allowed me to administer the last rites to a production without fear. There would still be depression, which was only natural, but now I quaintly thought of those periods as simple decompression, where I acclimatised to the rhythm of my domestic life, whilst inwardly training for the rigours of the next film; spending no exertion at all, for the hard work had already happened in committing to the next project. Deciding was the most challenging part – a project or idea I could live with for the two years it would take to complete – after that, all I needed was to see it through. What I had not factored in was how much family life had changed me, so that I preferred to shoot as close to my home town as possible; how I needed to sleep in my own bed with my husband and child; and to live a life without phones, flights or meetings. I wanted a summer of soccer camps and theme parks, anything that kept my child joyful and my husband happy with his choices. If that came at the expense of certainties and trajectories, then so be it. This was what had been promised and what was wanted, but the sense of dread I felt as post-production on *The Folded Leaf* wrapped was palpable. When we lost close to half an hour on the edit because Gabi and our backers had argued that the first cut was prohibitively long for international distributors, I was relieved because it gave me another month to work on the film. With older productions, I had raged and argued to the point of war for the right to cut the film to the length that suited my vision. Now, I agreed almost straight away, calculating how much extra time that would give me. Four more weeks to play at being a director. After that, who knew? I held on to Cosima's book because it haunted me and would continue to do so. Already I felt it taking over in my mind, as previous stories had done. There is a way that stories come to you, percolating with existing ideas, before they coalesce into a newly defined form that cannot be explained. I'd remained in the headspace for *The Folded Leaf*, reluctant to leave, and now the arrival of this novel was pulling me away and I went readily. In that context, my walk with Cosima was its physical expression: the march towards an idea; back to certainties and away from the cliff edge. There would be a long period of development, one which I would alternatively love and get frustrated with, which meant I could work from home. I would probably have a full year at home before shooting, giving me the space to be with my family, so long as I remained aware of the time I needed to give. There would be rows and accusations, but in themselves they would not be fatal so long as I explained my case. Suddenly *The Folded Leaf* became less a film to hold on to, but one to be thrust on to others. I had done my part. By the festival's end, it would be down to outside agents, and the fear of that lost its former potency. I was emerging from an extended period of mourning back into the living world. The sensation felt new to me every time, so in those final yards towards the hotel, I was filled with wonder and gratitude that those processes and emotions had come back; how as an artist, I was still capable. Can I offer you a lift back to your apartment? I asked. There are drivers at our disposal if you're in a hurry. It's fine, maestro, she said. I like to walk at this hour. It's good for my circulation and my thoughts. Also, I have a meeting with a museum donor not too far from here shortly. I'm going to wander to bide my time. You always feel safe to walk around the city? I asked. It's still early. If you are a *flâneur*, maestro, then I'm a *flâneuse*, she replied. Walking is what gives me life, and what stimulates my ideas. These streets echo with the sound of walking women, from those employed in manual labour to those who work in other ways. I would never give up the right to claim the streets as my own, whether I walk at seven a.m. or after midnight. This is a basic freedom for all women, whether they choose to walk or not. If men don't have to make this choice, then neither should I. Again she astonished me, and it made our connection clearer, beyond the shared references and cultural sympathies dictated by our age: the work of our feet and the sense that came from moving them; the freedom to always be on the move. We had the other's measure now, and again I was overcome with thankfulness. I couldn't imagine not working with Cosima on the project. You seem very cheerful for someone who started the day at dawn service, she said. When we left the church, it felt like we were going to a funeral. It's the growing light, I said, it lifts my spirits. But it was also the ascension of ideas, and for now that remained unsaid.

6.

Tom was reading his phone in the lobby, his identity swallowed by the plushness of the sofa and the nook he had chosen. He was learning how to blend in, so that recognition did not impede his ability to get out and do things. On our walks now, I noticed how his movements mirrored Lorien: he moved quickly, and on crowded streets kept his head down. Only when the environment was clearer did he allow himself to slacken, taking in everything he needed to, so that his concessions remained gentle nuisances rather than something more prohibitive. With further movies, he would have to reconsider that, but for now he was free and open to the world. His face gave no sign of the night's exertions; the simple recovery of youth that is as fleeting as the beauty it hosts. He'd given no explanation on what had happened with Lorien and I knew it was not my business to ask. It would be down to what was said and how they revealed themselves through their bodies as we worked through the day: a word or touch which clarified or dispelled. Nothing in his frame spoke of who he was waiting for either: Lorien, Gabi or myself. Or maybe none of us, finding the only way to secure privacy was in the shadow of a crowded room such as this. The more I thought about it, the more obvious it became that he wanted to be alone; how this might be his only time in a day loaded with commitments. As I was about to return to my room, his phone rang, and the illumination in his face revealed the deliverance he'd been waiting for. I had stared at that face for months, during the shooting and editing of the film, and even now there were still landmarks of expression that were new to me. I would have photographed him just then if I could; one further carat to be mined. Hey, maestro, he called, the phone call finished, his demeanour moving from rapturous to wicked. I saw you coming in out the corner of my eye, he said. You were just hovering. I didn't know whether you wanted to be alone, I said. You looked deep in thought. No one sits in a hotel lobby wanting to be alone, he laughed. This is a room for attention seekers. Although I thought we were meeting for breakfast until the concierge told me that you'd gone out. Did you forget? I needed a walk to wake me up a little, I said. Ended up reaching as far as the Duomo. That's pretty far, he said. You know me, I said, I like to get my thoughts together before we spend the day explaining ourselves. Ah, don't remind me, he said. Is this going to be painful? It won't be as technical as yesterday, I said, but they'll want a lot. Sorry that I made you wait. Happy to eat now, if you like.

He waved the suggestion away, regressing to a farmland teenager as he buried himself into a corner of the couch. I'm gonna have to pass, maestro. I ended up working out and then sat in the dining room with my lonely buffet for one. The local salami was very good, by the way. So it's my turn to be lonely now, is that it? I joked. I can stay for a quick coffee, he said, but then I have to split. Have an errand to run with one of the translators before the interviews start. That was them on the phone? I asked. Yeah, he said. This one's turned into my Italian fixer. She's really helpful. Will you tell her about last night? I asked. As much as she wants to be bored with, he said, with his face suggesting he wished it were as little as possible. When he stood up to follow me into the dining room I registered his striped sweatshirt. It belonged to Lorien, who'd worn it often during downtime on set. You traded in the Gucci for something warmer, I said. What, this? he asked, blushing. Lorien had it lying around. Thought I might as well borrow it. The sweater was twice his size but suited him well, the excess fabric falling loosely from his shoulders and hanging close to his knees. I had never worn my husband's clothes, nor he mine. Very early on, I'd taken his underwear on a shoot to see whether a stretch of fabric in my hands would somehow keep me closer to him, but I ended up being too busy to even unpack it. There had never been a relationship in my youth where a lover's property was mine to take. I could never be as free. The simple act of wearing your lover's shirt or sweater was unknown to me, a layer of intimacy that was never conferred by those I had cherished. I had their books and their cameras, records and old videos, but not clothes. I could never wear their touch around my neck in a scarf, tighter across the waistband and arse in their jeans, or as loosely as Tom wore Lorien's sweatshirt, for I was of a different tribe, and our path to happiness had been a long-winding one of discovery, setbacks, shame and covert behaviour, before we learned to speak with our art, and from that saw how we must be out-spoken about our lives in the wider world. As he walked ahead of me I could see that it meant both nothing and everything. He walked with a magic unbeknown to others, and the buttoned-down joy in that made my heart sing. They learned from our mistakes, the kids now. They would not be afraid. If you're hanging around, said Tom, can you do me a favour? Can you wake Lorien at eight? He's switched his cell off and unplugged the room phone. Blame the alco-hol from last night. Just the alcohol? I asked. We had a joint afterwards, he said. It wasn't very strong weed, but it knocked him out pretty quick. I suggested that he speak to the front desk or, failing that, to Gabi. Neither of those will work, he said, you know how he gets in the morning. If the first sound he hears is someone hammering on his door he'll be in a shitty mood until lunchtime. Tom was exaggerating, but there was truth in what he said: Lorien had to work harder than we did to keep his mornings agreeable. On set he was focused; the extra work lay in what it would some-times take to get him there, factoring in staggered call times and more conducive breakfasts. He was not difficult to work with first thing, mostly silent or abrupt until he reached speed, but I wondered whether the events of last night had set him on a fiercer path. Tom's look was a warning of an encroaching mood to keep at bay. He had visions three hours into the future, and did not want any camera to pick up on that, however minutely. You're actors, I wanted to say to him. Your schools trained the life out of you. When the camera turns over you leave all your shit behind. You'll fake it for this junket the same as you do for the entertainment channels in Hollywood, answering the questions that tire you out with million-dollar smiles on your faces. But I could not be so flippant when I was reminded of Lorien's brief slip of fatalism before the car turned up to drive us back from the factories. Whereas Tom would share, there was much that he kept to himself. He had honesty and openness, and the willingness to work hard, yet I was aware of this reserve, which if not entirely hidden, was not readily acknowledged. If I give you his room key, you can get in there and give him a nudge. If he's up at eight, he'll have an hour to himself before the grooming and styling at nine. I'll be back by then. You have his room key? I asked. He cut me a duplicate. I did the same with my room. Makes things easier, you know? All this knocking on doors and bruising my pretty hands. There was a look that passed between us that spoke of more than just last night. It flashed across their week together so far, of snatched moments and room visits. I thought of Tom sleeping in Lorien's room because he was unable to reach that state on his own. He was rested and happy to be working hard; content with the people around him and the future stemming from that. It rang out from his oversized sweater and the easy way he slid the room key into my palm. You know the room number, right? he asked. 206. His phone buzzed twice, knocking against his coffee cup, and amplifying the demands on his time. That's the translator. I'll be back for grooming. Quick as I can. It was seven thirty. I finished my breakfast in the dining room before I walked the stairs to the second floor. Lorien's room was on the other side of the palazzo, overlooking the walled garden. I thought of Tom looking out on to that garden as Lorien slept from his weed lullaby; whether he saw the green shoots pushing through frozen soil, or whether he was in a haze of his own, living his dream as he watched over Lorien. I stood in the stubby corridor that linked bed and bath before venturing forward. It was ten minutes to eight and I was wary of a bullish entrance, switching on the full lights and briskly pulling back the curtains. I was neither his nanny nor his maid and how I would wake him gave me pause for thought. You could have friendships that last for decades, supporting each other through all of life's stages, lovers, marriages, the birth of children and the passing of parents, but through all that, sleep, deep night sleep, remained an unknown. An artist several years ago had created an installation series comprising single twenty-minute films of various people who wielded power engaged in deep sleep. She asked CEOs, politicians, writers, actors and campaigners, athletes, tech giants and landowners. I was a name who made the original list, and I turned the request down, and not just because of my longstanding belief that I did not belong on the other side of the camera, that I could not acquiesce the power of my eye to submit to the gaze of others. It was partly due to a conversation I had with my husband who adamantly vetoed the idea. I don't believe that art should have boundaries, he said, but I believe in the power of choice. I get it. What this artist wants to do is break down the fourth wall. It's valid, but there are questions of privacy for us to consider. Our own red lines. Remember those? In being filmed sleeping, people'll see what I see, and so in breaking your privacy, you also break mine. Those who need the affirmation that badly can take up her offer. They can fill their boots for all I care, but leave something of yourself just for your family. Even after that, I secretly deferred for the next few days. I would have turned down the offer instinctively, but it had arrived at a low point between films when I was questioning my bravery and looking for ways to reinvigorate it. The offer was attractive financially and beneficial to my ego; every list was subjective, but the recognition that I had power was at the time important to hear, for I was firmly of the belief that I had none, exhausted and invisible. But my instinct to remain the observer rather than observed was the strongest one, and for this reason, I declined. Maybe there was something of jealousy in my refusal also; my wish to pull a camera before a sleeping actor rather than her. But then, in *Daguerréotypes*, Agnes Varda filmed a sequence with a sleeping butcher that was in turn intimate and contrived, so perhaps she beat us all to it. If I thought of a camera being between Lorien and myself, for example, then it made the intrusion easier. It would frame the context of our exchange and give reason to why I was there rather than Tom. The fantasy of this propelled me into the bedroom but I could only get as far as one of two easy chairs positioned by the window. Lorien slept, while I sat in the near dark; a snatch of daylight breaking above the curtain rail. He was covered, so I could only make out his shape under the duvet and his face was turned away from me. Only his tangled hair was visible, from the additional glow of light under the bathroom door, and a stray foot, hanging down the side of the bed. He slept on the right side, closest to me, rather than the middle, a stack of pillows scrunched to his left, indicating that Tom had slept there, at least for a while. Again, I questioned why Tom wanted to make me aware of this, and in such a direct way. Was I his intimate or his confessor? When Lorien finally turned, I saw someone in the throes of manhood, but whose youth still threatened to usurp that; the softness of his unlined face and the furious pursing of his lips giving a che-rubic air. Awake he looked older than his years, marked by experience and a projection of confidence that made anyone in his orbit feel instantly comfortable. He was friendly and had no ego, despite the effort of others to build such an aura around him. It went beyond straight talking and unvar-nished generosity, more a question of loyalty and trust, both what he gave and what he inspired. He was a man it was impossible not to love. The innocence of his pose made me think of my child, who I watched sleeping most nights, and could not imagine a time when I would no longer do so. Our miracle boy, beautiful, loving, and often trying; still the centre of our world, giving further enrichment to the union with my husband. Against the odds, personal, societal and practical, we had created a family and were living the life we had separately, covertly, wished for. At least once over the course of the night I would wake to check up on our boy, to satisfy my peace of mind, but also my curiosity of this wondrous alien who was both part of us and a person of his own making. The dreams we had for him. Everything I was unable to say aloud for fear of him batting my sentimentality away, expressed through my hand stroking his head or rearranging his bedcovers. The chair I sat on in his bedroom, as here, on the right-hand side of the bed close to the window, was my favourite view in the house. I prized the atmosphere of the kitchen where we spent most of our time, and the peace of my study had given me a stable place I had long fought for, wished for, but my son's room, and the sound of his breathing as he slept, was what I carried with me everywhere, and the knowledge that without it, our home was only half-built. It was Lorien who woke by himself as I was in the depth of my thoughts, his body shifting and eyes slowly opening before focusing on me. Should I ask you what you're doing here? he said. Tom asked me to give you an alarm call, I said, holding up the room key. But I wasn't quite sure how I was going to do that. You looked so peaceful. That boy worries too much, he said. I'm a grown-up. I know when to get out of bed. I'll leave you to it, I said, rising. You need some time to yourself before we get started. Stay awhile, maestro, while I gather my marbles, he said. It's odd, but it's nice having you here. What's the time? Just turned eight, I said. You see, he smiled, no matter how wasted I get, my body clock never lets me down. I have faith in my methods. He shifted on to his side so that he could better see me. Where's Tom? He had an errand to run, I said. He didn't say what it was, but there was something cheeky in his eye. He took a driver? asked Lorien. No idea, I said. All I know is that he went somewhere with the translator. Oh, OK, Lorien rolled on to his back and stared at the ceiling. I guess we'll see him when we see him. Do you want to fix us a couple of espressos? There's a machine over there. He pointed to a dark corner close to the bathroom, where a pod machine sat atop a dresser. I stood up and reached for the nearest lamp light as I walked, but he held up his hand. Don't, he said. Getting up is one thing, dealing with the light, another. Pull the bathroom door open if you need a little more. He shook the covers off and sat up, reaching for the bottle of water on his nightstand. The shadow from the bathroom door hit the side of his face and chest as I pulled it ajar, sculpting him further so that his already muscular body appeared even more defined. The stretch and pull of the muscles in his throat as he downed the full bottle, the thickness of his gasp as he drew breath, rivulets of water spilling down his chin and on to his belly, the fierce beating of his chest afterwards. Fuck, he said, I needed that. In shadow he was no longer a boy, the depth of his tone and ferocity of breath suddenly older and rooted in the basic needs of our Neolithic forebears. He had thirst so he drank. His body was hot, so he was naked beneath the covers. The simplicity in giving the body what it needed; his reactions and impulses ever changing, so that I knew that if I shot him now he would be completely different to how he had appeared in my film; all from a shift of light, and the observation that followed. This was my life, the observer in the shadows; watching life but somehow not being part of it; how film was an accumulation of observation, a simulation of all that you'd seen or dreamed. There would be a film years from now when I would light the scene to match the shadow and fog of Lorien's room; how the import of that moment stayed with me until I had the right opportunity to replicate it elsewhere. This is what the creative mind taught you, what to store and when to reveal, memories maturing, morphing and disintegrating in their compartmentalised space. Maestro, he called, can you throw me another bottle of water, please? There's a couple left in the minibar under the coffee machine. I took two small bottles and walked over with them. I can't throw in this light, I said. If one of them hits your face, I'd never hear the end of it. Imagine turning up to our interviews with a black eye. Gabi would be livid. Lorien laughed. And my agent. They're protective bastards, aren't they? Treat you like racehorses when your stars are aligning, and then you're no better than farm animals when those stars fade. You'll still a racehorse, I said. I can assure

you of that. Thanks, maestro, he said, grinning. A flattered
ego and enough water to flush my toxins away. I'll be a new
man by breakfast. I nodded towards the outline of the book
pile on his nightstand. What are you reading? Pick them up
here? No, at the Strand in New York last week. Tom was
reading for some producer so I tagged along for a couple of
days. Second callback so he was nervous about it. You know
how he gets. I do, I said, something tells me he'll never lose
that. He cares about what he's doing too much. So I got
these, he gestured. Bassani, *The Garden of the Finzi-Continis*,
and *After the Divorce* by Grazia Deledda. He spoke airily, but
with a nod in my direction that suggested his desire for
approval. You're reading Italian novels now? I asked. I'm sure
you have us Americans down as burger-eating primitives,
he laughed, but some of us do read books from time to time.
I think nothing of the sort and you know it, I said, smiling.
Without William Maxwell, we wouldn't have a film, or the
opportunity to be here. That's true, he said. He had serious
chops, that guy. The Deledda was my mother's suggestion,
actually. When I asked her about Italian novels, it was one
of the titles she thought of. They didn't have the others, but
I lucked out with this. I picked up the books, both well-
thumbed softcovers, their wear indicating several lives lived
before reaching Lorien's hands. Even at arm's distance they
already smelled of him, a mix of sandalwood, leather and
musk. So what did you think? I asked. In the case of Bassani,
it's a book about death, he said, at least to my mind. Others
would say it's about first love, I said, their initial response, at

least. Oh, it is that, he said, but I was mostly struck that it was a book of endings. That the outcome hangs heavily over the course of the book. A bit like our film. He starts by taking you to a mausoleum and tells you that most of the characters in the book will die in the holocaust, making that stone palace a dream to be unfulfilled. It also makes you appreciate the life in the rest of the book, no? I said. The difficulty and pain of young love, its complications and mis-understandings. Sure, he said, all the unknowns that get your heart racing and brain working. I've never worked harder to understand that than in my current situation. The book speaks to me from that point of view. But this is what I'm left with, maestro, what I think about. The difficulty of being happy when you know that it will end. It was the feeling I had during the entirety of our shoot. How there was an expiration date on the good work we were doing. The summer would end and I'd move on to a new film and a new set of relationships. Only I wasn't ready to say goodbye to this particular family. So what to do, barricade myself in my room and refuse to come on set in order to stretch the experience out, if only by a day? Or suck it up and let these novels absorb me? I choose the novels every time. Let those characters fuck up so I don't have to. I thought about the last fortnight of filming when everyone in the crew was aware of our time drawing to a close, and how that gave rise to tensions and petty squabbles as we all fought against it. Lorien remained agreeable on set, but away from it seemed angry and distant, taking meals in his room and no longer socialising with the rest of the cast. I let him be, for it was not my place to tell him how to behave. Only when I sensed that he was withdrawing on set, giving less in order to feel less, did I intervene, pulling him aside as a shot was being prepared. There were no raised voices but we did speak frankly, and after that order was restored. Did you see the movie they made of *Finzi-Continis*? he asked. I'd be totally surprised if you hadn't. It's a classic, I said, one of those films you see that makes you want to become a better filmmaker. I first saw it in a cinema in Warsaw when I was a student. We'd travelled to the city for a weekend to take part in some protest or other, and I noticed a poster advertising a revival for it as we headed to the demonstration. I blamed it on the size of the crowds later, but I deliberately slipped off so that I could watch it. That's such a maestro move, he laughed. Kudos for that. Did you admire it as much as I did? Very much so, I said, and I wasn't expecting to. I was nineteen and was trying to get away from mannered families and their pristine houses. All the social niceties you lived with for so long and now wanted to rebel against. I came from a modest background, and that's the polite way of putting it, but there were still strict social conventions that ruled our household. We ate dinner as a family every night, went to church on Sundays and feast days, and saw our grandparents at the weekend. I knew nothing of the book. It was the director Vittorio De Sica I was interested in. So when I realised it was about tennis and tea parties I almost walked out. But then the power of storytelling took over. When this is in harmony with film photography, you get magic, and that's what I saw. The wonder of the present before a lament for the dead. In a strange way, it was more political than attending the demonstration I was supposed to be at. Stayed with me longer, also. I saw it last week, said Lorien. On the plane with Tom. It pulled at me, for sure, but all the time I was thinking, Man, this is ripe for a remake. Really? I asked. Some films don't need to be tampered with. They're perfect as they are. Surely the history of film is built upon the arrogance of those who think they can improve on perfection, Lorien argued. Even if they're massive failures. No story is ever finished. From the Bible to the adaptation of this novel. Even William Maxwell's novel while we're on the subject! It's all fair game. Hollywood is out of its mind, I said, always has been. And as for Maxwell, there wasn't a film before ours so it's not the same thing. What would you say if someone wanted to remake one of your films? he asked. They wouldn't dare, I said. I own all the rights, so they'd have a time trying. I recall when my second film was a hit, there was talk of making an English-language version for American audiences. I think I entertained the option for no longer than an afternoon. Once you allow people to tamper with your vision there's no turning away from that. You have to live with those decisions. I was thinking more of you remaking *Finzi-Continis*, he said. Can't you see it? The potential to tell that story in a new way? There's some films that can't be improved upon, I said. This is one. Why don't you try, Lorien? I know my limits, he said. I'm a show pony who looks good and trots out my lines the best I can. I'll stick to my lane. You can be more, I said. You are more. Believe that. It would take too much, Lorien said. More than I want to give. Here's the thing. You can live in your head or you can be happy. Too much of life is given to analysis. I agree with that, I said, more than you realise. That's not to say I want to live blindly, maestro, more that you have to give yourself up to the day in order to live it. I learned a lesson from reading that novel. You're not always in control of when and how things end. What you can control is whether you embrace the moment. I have and I will. Is this about how things are developing with Tom? I asked. Nothing gets past you, he laughed. Partly, but it applies to everything. The roles I take, the person I want to be. Big stuff and small stuff. I handed him the espresso still burning my hand. Reading gives you freedom, I said. You become a different person when you talk about books. He laughed. Hollywood wants you to appear smart while in reality being completely dumb. Look pretty, hit your mark, and don't ask difficult questions. No one's interested in any deeper thought. Do you think I talk with another director the way I'm talking to you now? All they care about is whether I still have my abs or how quickly I can bulk up if a meathead part calls for it. They're bothered about whether you hold your fuck appeal, and if that's strong enough to open a movie convincingly over a holiday weekend. Also, a desire that I keep my queerness in check. My ability to give them something to feel on screen is neither here nor there. Did our

summer together really make you that cynical? I asked. Not
that, he said, just rethinking my priorities and the jobs I take.
If I don't feel passionate about a project, I don't care who's
attached to it or how good it might be for me, I'm just not
doing it. That fire you have, I said. The only other time
you're close to that is when the camera turns or . . With
Tom? he asked. That would be right, maestro. We're not
going to do anything stupid, but I don't give a fuck what
anyone else thinks. I don't give a fuck either, I said, imitating
him, other than it makes me happy. You're in paradise. Not
quite, he said. Did you see how he blew up at me last night?
Over the scarf? I don't always get it right. I mistake our ease
for an understanding we don't yet have. But I'm in it for
something greater. Don't know the shape of it, and yet. And
yet? I repeated. It's worth the risk, he said. Even if he thinks
I bully him sometimes. He reached for my hand and grabbed
it hard. Means a lot, he said. Your approval. Drink your
coffee and let's get ready to tackle the day, I said, patting the
bed. Game faces. Too right, he said. We'll get through these
fucking interviews and make the most of them. They're fun
sometimes, if they choose some decent people to talk with
you. Those guys we saw yesterday were OK. Bit serious, but
OK. Today's pick should be lighter. That's what I told Tom,
I said. The scale of these junkets is new to him. By the end
of the day he'll be as sick of them as we are, said Lorien. I
guarantee it. You have to forgive me, maestro. I'm an angry
bastard at this time of the morning. He leaned forward with
his empty cup. Another one of these will help, though. He

walked behind me, pulling on a robe. I'm gonna jump in
the shower. I'll see you in an hour, right? A grip on my
shoulder and then he was gone, the thunder of the shower
head and the heaviness of water in the air. I felt the disparity
between Hollywood and Europe in that moment; a dismissal
or indication that he had shared as much as he had the stomach for. I was no more than a serf, or a lesser angel tending
unreliable gods. I knew should the situations be reversed, I
would rip out my heart and guts in an offering to those I
trusted. I came from emotional stock, and this element from
my family genealogy was present in all my work, putting on
the line what I sometimes felt unable to say elsewhere.
Lorien's feelings, his desire, could long play below the surface, and he was happy for it to stay that way. Being
submerged was what kept him going. He was right in that
he took every opportunity, but he swam rather than jumped
for it. I made the espresso and placed it on his nightstand.
Before I left, I paged through the Bassani novel for a last
time, wanting to see whether he had written any notes or
scored passages as he read, as he was wont to do. His script
had been littered with notes over the course of shooting, as
if confirming or debating every note or character direction.
He made it look easy, but he worked for every line. I found
what I was looking for at the end of the opening chapter, the
one that had resonated so much. Under the elegiac passage
about the lost mausoleum, was his familiar penmanship, a
capitalised scrawl: T + ME. WHAT I WANT.

7.

There were to be photos taken before the morning's interviews, in the form of a press call outside the palazzo. I always
dreaded these moments, finding them a forensic study of the
worst kind. A photo call lacked the grace of a movie camera,
concerned only with the aggression of the moment – the
micro-moment – which yielded a sellable shot. There were
thirty photographers waiting to attack, penned in a corner
of the palazzo courtyard, where we were expected to stand
before a festival-branded backdrop and submit. We were led
out one at a time, Tom and Lorien separately, before I joined
them for a series of group shots. The photographers had been
sent in their number for pictures of the boys, Lorien particularly, following the wider success of his last two films. I was
under no illusions as to the nature of my role – to legitimise
their presence as actors – but should I feel any outrage about
that, it was made clear that I should suffer it silently, for our
publicist took no prisoners. We were all at the mercy of her

schedule and demands. It was the first time I'd seen a party of this size in the walled garden, in some way making sense of the layout and space: the boxy planting around the perimeter leading to two sets of steps in the middle which gave way to a mixture of mature plants and oversized stone urns circling a sunken stone pool. We were to stand on the steps leading to the water, as if making an offering to the gods who would bless our film. I'd not seen the boys since our haphazard breakfasts, having been in a Skype meeting with my editor, Stjepan, who was flying in late that afternoon. We'd discussed what was happening with some of the footage we still felt we had use for, either for a longer cut later down the line or to review more urgently if I felt something was still missing following tonight's screening. It had only happened once before, after a premiere with great fanfare at Cannes; I'd returned home with my statue and together with Stjepan recut the composition of one scene which had gnawed at me with its unevenness. It was a scene of a woman arranging flowers into a vase while talking to an unseen visitor outside; a conduit to a more demanding exchange, it was still of great importance. Water cannot flow upstream, and I was painfully aware at Cannes of the editorial knots I had tangled myself in with that particular minute of film. The audience were none the wiser, so enchanted were they with the actress playing the lead, her sonorous voice and the glide of her hand as she reached to place each flower. When I was asked about the change by one hawk-eyed critic, the same one who had walked out of my film years before, I said it was because I was so close to perfection, I would have been at fault had I not corrected it. I never believe my films are perfect, I said, more imperfect experiments, but when you realise that you have risen as high as the sun, possibly for the first and last time, you do everything within your power to reach it. I would never speak in those terms again, but the final version of that scene gave a more coherent flow to that moment, and so respecting the actress and the audience. Until *The Folded Leaf*, that film was the closest I had to a masterpiece. Others would add another six of my films to join it — a list of higher work — but they knew nothing. There was another film which I would reshoot and edit completely if I could: one of the crowed-about masterpieces on which I reluctantly concurred. It was a film about a husband and wife following their only child to a new town after her surprise marriage and the tragedy that came from that. I worked on it less than two months after the death of my parents, who had passed from their illnesses in short succession. Every frame was lit and shot in such a way as to compress all emotion, each character closed down to the point of physical pain. I had never demanded such masochistic performances from my actors before; in many ways, it felt like emotional torture with no reasoning or end point, an insult to the humanity of my parents. It remains one of my most decorated and requested prints, but I am unable to watch it now, for I knew I had the ability to change things at the time, in order to protect myself and my actors, but I did nothing because I thought it made a better film.

Subsequently, a recut was never far from my mind and the team I had around me knew to prepare. I embraced the fact that the possibility existed should I need to. While I still owned the film before it was sold to a distributor, I had this small window of freedom, which I held on to like a crutch in more anxious moments. I did not see the boys until we were waiting in the dining room ready to be led outside. Something in their stature had changed, how they stood and the eye contact they held with each person in the room. They were energetic and friendly, jumping on the spot to gee themselves up, flirting and laughing with the publicist so that she knew she could trust them to take instruction. I was in my black suit, which had been pressed overnight, along with some gifts the publicist had left in my room: an Armani T-shirt; a McQueen skull scarf which I immediately took to, the punk in me, and a pair of triple monk shoes with safety-pin buckles. She sent a hairdresser and make-up artist to appraise me while I finished the call to my editor. I did not quite look like an ageing supermodel, more that I could stand next to my handsome boys without letting myself down. I thought of my husband, who would approve of the shoes and make subtle comments on how I should dress like that more often. I watched as Lorien was led out to the pack. Good morning, he said with a smile, nodding as he took his mark before the backdrop. A fine day for it. Thanks for coming out. Then he looked at the bank of cameras and held his gaze. He stood with his legs slightly apart, his hands in his jacket pockets, which gave his shape a protean symmetry and strength. He hid nothing, which somehow allowed you to look even more. From the low murmur that emanated while we were waiting inside, the pack's noise immediately switched to a deafening row as they forgot their coffee and pastries, their small talk and gossip, and bowed to their instincts. The din from rapid-fire shutters and the unrelenting bombing of flash bulbs – cluster bombing in an Italian garden – and over that, the incessant shouting, as each photographer called for Lorien's attention. Look up to your right, Lorien! Down right, Lorien. Look in the middle, Lorien. Blue eyes! Bottom row! Bottom row! He was flustered by none of it, meticulously shifting his gaze from one side of the photo line to the other: above, below and centre. He changed his position a couple of times, crossing his arms before letting them fall softly by his side, but remaining strong at all times; handsome, compliant, capable, and vaguely other-worldly; the definition of a movie star. Man, I'm gonna mess this up, said Tom in my ear. I've done a couple of these before, but not with this amount of photographers. They're animals. Jesus. Just remember to be polite, I whispered. And breathe. They're not there to humiliate you, just to get a good picture. Think of it as your school photo to the Nth power. Nth power, I like that, he said. Makes it sound less anxiety ridden. We continued to watch Lorien at work. He was enjoying it a little more now, joking with the photographers as they yelled their instructions. I don't speak English any more, he said, only Italian. We shot a movie here so I'm fluent now. The photographers roared their approval and complied, enjoying the game. Lorien grinned and continued to hit his mark. He makes it look so easy, said Tom. How does he do that? By not resisting it, I guess, I said. Same as you do with a film camera. But I trained myself not to look at the film camera, he laughed. That's the point of film acting. Here, you can only look at the camera. They'll pounce if you try anything else. Man, this is awful. Remember when we took the scooters out one night, I said, and you had to learn to hold the road no matter how your bodyweight shifted? Think of this as something similar. But we remained painfully aware of how time had slowed. Lorien had stood for no longer than five minutes, but we felt the impact of every exposure as he did his job. Tom exhaled deeply as the publicist walked towards him, and in the breath that followed, transformed. He put his arm around my shoulder and punched me affectionately. Watch me do this. I'll look corny but I'll still slay it. And then in a louder voice as he was being led away: I have to tell you about my errand, he said, smiling wildly, summoning the character he would present outside. The mural! I've seen it! And with a wink he was gone. Gabi joined me as we watched Tom get the best of his situation, mirroring Lorien with his hands in his pockets, but switching his expression between smile and pose. He radiated energy and the pleasure of being there, which the line appreciated and fed upon. Their demands continued, but with less ferocity, for Lorien was the bigger draw. He remained in the courtyard, standing with the publicist at the side of the photo bank, and it was

clear to me that his presence gave Tom strength and encouragement, pointing him out every few shots, with a laugh.
How am I doing compared to this guy? he asked. *Bene? Molto
bene?* He glanced up to the second floor, Lorien's bedroom,
and laughed to himself, before looking sideways to see
whether he had noticed. He was subtle, glancing upwards as
if wanting to feel the sun on his face, but I knew it was an
acknowledgement of the sanctity of that room and of his
desire to return there. When I joined them on the steps, it
was the insistent ripple from the water feature that struck me
the most, seeming to run through the battery of noise facing
us. I imagined the running water rushing past our feet and
lapping at those of the photographers; the rise and fall of the
tide depending on how we were falling in and out of favour.
It's strange how in situations that feel entirely artificial, my
senses would always reach for what was natural, in this case
the water, and the intermittent sun as it broke through
patches of cloud. This is making me want to go for a piss, I
said. It's all that coffee. My words had the desired effect, of
making the pair of them break into laughter. The ability to
do so is one of the great joys of life. I thought of my husband
and child giggling in our kitchen, and that of the boys most
evenings as we relaxed after a day on set. Speak under your
breath, said Lorien. You can never trust these guys not to
lip-read. Knowing our luck this is being filmed also, so the
less they can make out, the better. I need a piss too now
you've said that, complained Tom. Man, you totally said the
wrong thing at the wrong time. Imagine what would

happen if the three of us pissed into that water feature, said Lorien, leaning into us. Very classic, with our backs to the camera and our heads slightly turned. You're lucky we rate this film, maestro. In other circumstances I'd do it, just to get a reaction. We sat on the steps, a concession to our rebellion and their boredom at our stagnating poses. Act natural, the publicist mouthed. Chat among yourselves. First rule of acting, said Tom under his breath as he caught her eye. Create chemistry where there is none. You saw the mural? I asked. How? I went back there, this morning, he said. While you guys were fooling around last night, I was taking pictures of the road name and the apartment frontage so that I would recognise it. I get that, I said, but how did you get in? My dad worked as a janitor for an office building during winter when things were slow on the farm, he said. One thing I know about janitors is that they get up early. What? I was trying to surprise you, he finished, as if reading my mind. Let's not get over-involved, said Lorien. We can talk about this when there aren't a truckload of people trying to work out what we're saying. He was standing now while the two of us sat on the lower steps, giving the air of a parent lecturing a child. I stood and folded my arms, so that there were two parents now, a nuclear family raising a precocious boy. Tom, for his part, made the most of the moment, stretching his legs out and looking up at us with glee. My teachers, he called out. You don't get better than these two. I wanted to talk, desperate to extract the full story from Tom while it was fresh in his mind. I recognised the haze that

flashed on his face as he mentioned the mural as being something close to mine following that afternoon in the garden
with Cosima; one that was in parts dreamy, rapturous,
bewildered and consumed. It gave me so much pleasure that
he had seen what I'd seen – I was happy for that – but there
was also uneasiness on my part, fearing the mural's secrecy
slipping from my grasp. If I had my way I would have taken
him to the bottom of the steps where we could sit at the
stone pool's edge and talk in private, but our publicist thundered towards us after instructing the photographers to wrap
up, simultaneously praising our efforts while ushering us
inside to the conference suites where our interviews were to
be held. I know who that guy is, said Tom. He's crazy good.
They used one of his paintings on a hip hop record last year.
You're full of surprises. When I think I know about you and
all your classical references, you pull out the cool card. What
cool card, enquired the publicist, both listening and not
listening, needing to fill the air and allow her voice to be
heard. Just art talk, I said quickly. Remind me who we're
seeing next? It was not that I wanted to dismiss her, more
that it hadn't crossed my mind how known the artist would
be in the culture now, for Cosima had played down his
relevance. I was so used to the romance of him being forgotten, and the quietness with which Cosima talked of him.
We spoke of the past in a way that was both nostalgic and
reverential; our tones veered from joy to regret, encompass-
ing the sadness for those who had passed from the same
period, for he was not the only loss either of us had known,

but also acknowledging in less elegiac moments, the wonder at how we had lived bravely and openly at such a young age, and the adventures it gave rise to. So to hear Tom speak of him, with wonder also, but in a way that felt removed from ours, jolted me in a way that I wasn't expecting. Hearing his name being spoken aloud – Bruno B – was like learning about him for the first time, as if he were unfamiliar and not of my time. I realised then that I wanted Tom to equally reveal more and never speak of him again. My possession was such that I was certain that whatever he said next would continue to feel this invasive. I felt almost violated on Cosima's behalf, and it was all of my making. I had taken them there. I had sent them the photographs. I recognised that this was jealousy, for if I had to explain in further detail how I had discovered the mural that would involve a discussion about Cosima, her story and her books. I realised in those moments how strongly I wanted to utilise the novel and the wider story around it for my next film, for the way I wished to hold it so close. I'm not a filmmaker who works in secrecy, but I only revealed the extent of my plans once the script had been fully formed. I frequently discussed passing interests, concepts and moods with Gabi and Stjepan so that they were aware of the direction of travel, but until the script was complete, I did not feel comfortable with sharing more widely beyond my husband, who was my sounding board and made sense in all things. This was the element of possession that making any art imbibed upon the practitioner: for as much as I loved Tom, the need for making this film was stronger, and so it felt necessary to hold the seeds of its origins closely. I wanted them sewn under my skin where they could leave no trace. I wished to wipe phone records and memories. It was shocking the lengths I felt I could go to in order to protect my developing thoughts on the film. Cosima was no such person, for it was her generosity which had led to the idea forming. Tom also, who only had fondness and gratitude for our experience. Neither were threats to me, so why did it feel so? Because to be an artist is to carry a sense of being embattled; how work can only be created if you feel that you are the only one who can do it. I had lost some early producers and collaborators with this attitude. Lovers had left me, and friends had washed their hands. I had not acted this way for a long time, before my marriage and a husband who straightened out my knots, but this particular story, and the sense of nostalgia it invoked within me, was twisting up all that good work. I could feel the hardening of my arteries and slowing of my blood flow, picturing myself three months from now, working solidly on the project to the detriment of everything else; pushing aside any functions or commitments, personal or professional, which were not deemed essential. I was known for my kindness on set, but this was where I was the bastard: figuring out the work and nailing it down. For the right to do that, I would give up everything. My memory of Tom was him giving me the thumbs-up as he and Lorien walked into their interview room – I was being led with Gabi into the suite opposite. It made me think of my son's innocence and how I would fight to the death to preserve that. Tom I would also protect, even at the expense of my film. I was soft now, my teeth crumbling into my jaw. Soon I would be old. I had fight in me, but not against those I loved. Marriage had changed my priorities, along with the quest for peace of mind. But still, this protectionist impulse remained, heating my blood and rising above more restrained argument. Every film had been a fight to overcome − either myself or the obstacles of others. I would leave behind a child on this earth, but my films would also remain, a testament to my determination to master how the eye coordinated the hand while translating the heart. In the same way, I needed to align my rituals on how I prepared with a spirit of openness. I would learn.

8.

Still, I persisted. How did you persuade the janitor to open up? I asked over lunch. Did you speak to him or the translator? She did, said Tom. I stood there and looked like butter wouldn't melt. I think she told him I was an actor and scholar of art in hip hop, and how this was an important piece I needed to catalogue for a film I was working on. Not quite sure what he swallowed of that story. Maybe none of it. She was wearing this animal-print sweater and he was staring at her tits the whole time. So the janitor walked you in? I asked. Yes, said Tom. After a little dance where we had to donate a hundred euros towards the upkeep of the mural. He said that if I knew the mural's significance, I would also appreciate how his unpaid dedication to keeping the work in the best condition possible was a lesson in love and respect, but that love costs. Ha, said Lorien. The dude fleeced you! And I suppose you didn't have any cash on you, as usual, leaving the poor translator to settle up. You're right, said Tom, but you don't have to be a dick about it. But he couldn't help himself from smiling as he spoke. They were jabbing and sparring, but still ready to kiss any bruises away. What's this record cover you were talking about? I asked, to which they both held up their phones. It's this guy, said Tom, pointing at his music library. The cover was a detail from a mural I hadn't seen before: a bear with a box head DJing on a set of turntables, where sparks flew. It was uplifting to see it: a yellow bear outlined in thick black, against a pink background. Through the phone's pixilation, I could still feel every line that came from his hand as he drew each form and then subsequently spray-painted over them. Was it from the train-track mural or elsewhere? Another question I needed to ask Cosima. I read some interview where the rapper said that he discovered him through a write-up of an old Keith Haring show in Paris, said Tom. The critic made out that our Italo graf dude Bruno was the nearest Haring would've had to a rival in Europe had he lived to produce enough work, and his interest piqued from that to dig out a piece to use for his record cover. I've got it on a T-shirt somewhere, I think. And this rapper's popular enough that you both have his music on your phones? I asked. Tom laughed. He's middle league, not big league. I downloaded it on to Lorien's phone to cut through all that singer-songwriter bullshit he has on there. That playlist was drier than a cracker until I mixed it up. He's like a toddler on Spotify, grinned Lorien. He only responds to crashes and beats. Helped you out, though, right? said Tom. The

Facebook interview earlier where you were waxing lyrical like a pro. They were lapping it up. It made a change from talking about the size of our penises, which is what they were trying to make us do, said Lorien. The scene where we come out of the swimming pool in our underwear, maestro, explained Tom. It's going to cause a ruckus. Seriously, said Lorien. So let me get this straight – he's dead and that's why you're interested in him? I get that he's talented – was talented – but is there some tragic story that you're being drawn to? A creative life that's cut short will always be a tragedy, I said. When I saw the mural yesterday, I was so moved by it. What did you think? It's nuts, said Tom. The energy and the amount of detail. It's aggressive, the way all graffiti is, but it also felt really sensitive. In one corner there's two small kids playing on a seesaw while their parent sits on a bench and reads the paper. It's city life, but also small-town life. I could've stared at just that small element for hours. Was the translator of the same mind? I asked. Oh, she didn't come out, said Tom, blushing. It was muddy out back and she didn't want to get her shoes dirty. Lord, keep my shoes clean, laughed Lorien. I've been a good girl and will not fall into temptation. What she did do was have a good chat with the janitor, said Tom, kicking him lightly, and then using the same foot to rub the spot. There's a woman that comes there three times a week to sit at the mural. Did you know this? She's the guide who took me, I said. I think it's part of her art tour of the city. Why would you look at the same painting almost every day when you're in a city where there's so much to see? asked Lorien. Sounds creepy to me. I feel that I know so little about art, said Tom, but I suppose the point is that it's impossible to see everything, so you end up returning to those pieces that resonate the most with you. In the farm town I grew up in, there was a postcard of a Jeff Koons installation on the library wall. A balloon dog tied to the base of an oversized hedge. I had no idea who had created it or where it came from, but it was the first thing I'd look for whenever I went there. When I finally saw the original at MoMA last year, I got the same feeling as looking at the mural. That I was simultaneously in the city and in my home town. And there was something really cool about that. I thought of the home that Tom would create years from now, whether with Lorien or someone else, and how it would mesh the sensibilities of his farmstead with everything he'd subsequently learned. He could live on the twentieth floor of a Manhattan tower and still bring a country air to it. He was proud that the solid elements of his background were not shaming; they had given him drive, openness and curiosity. Lorien had a similar drive, but he was constantly remaking himself. On the surface, his confidence flowed; only out of sight did his feet move furiously. There was something of me in both boys, which was why I wanted to warn them of my mistakes: the danger of your openness being taken advantage of, and of the damage to your body and mind from constantly running. In the middle was a still point, and the trick was to find and hold on to that. If Tom is your still point, don't let him go, I wished to say to Lorien. And to Tom: If your lover's search for knowledge does not match yours, walk away and don't look back. These were not my words to say, yet still they sat on my lips. What united my films was their search for a still point, successfully or otherwise. The janitor said something interesting about the woman who visited, Tom said. There's one night a year when she sleeps under the mural. It's happened twice now, he thinks. It could be more often, but he's started seeing a widow in town, so doesn't sleep in the basement as often as his employers think. He told you all that? I asked. Well, to the translator, Tom replied. I was too busy getting my shoes dirty looking at the mural. Doesn't that strike you as odd, her sleeping under it? Not unless there was some significance, I said. An anniversary or marker of some kind. It did not sound like the Cosima I was getting to know; the one who had rationalised her grief. She was not capable of being so impulsive, for she had cried all her impulses away. But then I thought of my parents and how the impact of their loss remained able to flay my skin to the bone, no matter the length of time that had passed, and in that moment, I saw her in a sleeping bag making a place for the night between the trees. The area had a vibe, said Tom. I sensed it as I walked through the courtyard. This patchy garden with some magic about it. No joke, it was everything you built it up to be. When there's treasure on every corner, you almost get used to finding public art that knocks you off your feet. This was like hitting the jackpot. I feel a bit left out by all this, said Lorien. When do I get to see this gift-of-life mural? I asked you at six a.m. and you told me to go fuck myself, remember? said Tom. Come on, man, said Lorien. I love you and everything, but six a.m. with a brandy hangover and this never-ending jetlag isn't the one. What? It's been up there for thirty-odd years, and you couldn't wait another few hours? They looked as if it was the first time each had heard the other's voice. Lorien was so casual with his declaration, aware that the atmosphere would change the moment he said it, but ploughing on regardless. His eyes, steely and bright, looked into Tom's. He would not run or shy away from what was so patently simple. Tom did not speak, only nodded, looking down at his hands, and then Lorien's hands, before reaching across the table to brush the hair from his face, a lightning gesture that reciprocated all that was offered. I remembered the need to speak the same truth to the man who became my husband, going to his place of work at the university and forcing my hands into my pockets to stop myself from banging on his classroom door. Instead, I stood at the back of the lecture hall and watched him speak, finding a space behind the back row, by the digital projector, which I patted as if it were a talisman. He was speaking about James Baldwin's poetry, reading stanzas from 'Paradise'. Let this be my summertime / Of azure sky and rolling sea, / And smiling clouds, and wind-kissed laughter, / And just myself entranced with thee. It was an example of the rare moment when we turn from opposing atoms to isotopes. I had previously declared my love into a void, but as I stood in the lecture hall I realised

that this would never be the case again, for I had found
someone of identical mind, proven by how that poem spoke
to and of me, declaring all that I had raced over there for.
Somehow, in a space outside of my understanding, my future
husband had taken the weather and knew that today was the
day. The poem was a gift, and one that I passed on now,
quietly repeating the stanza from the same poem that pulled
hardest on my chest. Let this be my happiness / 'Midst the
earth's swift-flowing woe. / Let this by my only solace – /
Just to know you love me so. They turned to look at me,
once again aware of my presence, their momentary bubble
becoming porous to the outside world. That's beautiful, said
Tom, rubbing his eye. Would you write that down for me,
please? I'd be happy to, I said. Sounds like Baldwin, right?
asked Lorien, to which I nodded. They gave us these poems
for background reading when I did a play in Chicago last
year. If the hope of giving / is to love the living, / the giver
risks madness / in the art of giving. It's from a poem called
'The Giver', I think. He was increasingly shy as he spoke, at
first certain of his gift, looking into Tom's face as he spoke,
and then away, his glance pitched downwards in carrying
the poem's weight. Better choice, I said. The vulnerability
of giving was also the reality of being alive to hope, and
although he looked bolstered by my encouragement and the
way that Tom's leg now wrapped around his under the table,
he was wiped out from the scale of effort; forgetting the
energy that bravery required. When can we get out of here?
he continued. Properly away. He wanted to be outside so

they could mark the moment somehow. The room was light-filled and bright, leading out on to a private section of garden, but it did not break the feeling of enclosure and the duties that were expected of them. Don't you ever feel like running away? he asked. I could get on a scooter and disappear for a few hours quite easily. Ride up the coast towards Piedmont. Maybe something more serious, like travelling down to France. I couldn't care less how many noses we put out of joint. We've got twenty minutes, said Tom, pointing to his phone. Then they own our asses for the next two hours. You can't live your life like a regular person in this business, said Lorien, smiling now. Everything you want to say or do must be deferred by two hours. If you weren't in this film how would we have met? asked Tom. Also, there'd be no girls screaming after you every twenty metres. Well, you have me there, said Lorien. I'm frustrated, but not so selfless as to lose my arrogance. Ha, said Tom, there's the old misery we know and love! Welcome back! I'm back, baby, said Lorien, with a high five. If we can't get out of here, let's at least rebel by finishing off this dessert they've left for us, Tom said. I don't think they're expecting us to demolish the lot, so let's surprise them. The dessert wine, too. Looks like there's enough for one small glass each. We can slouch on the interview sofas with our bellies out and insist that they frame us from the shoulders up. A trio of fat gastronomes on tour, laughed Lorien as he reached for the wine. Perfect suggestion. I would remember the lunch we ate that afternoon for many years, referencing the same menu in a later film because of the celebration it signalled: crostini, followed by a light chicken broth with poached eggs, ossobuco alla Milanese – braised shin of veal – served atop a saffron risotto, and pears baked in Marsala. I used it as a wedding dinner for an elderly couple who leave their disapproving families in Perugia and elope up north to Lombardy. They find each other late in life but are certain of their intentions and cannot wait for convention to keep up with their pace. It was a scene that gave further structure to the film – all that followed hung from the wedding dinner – but also wove my personal history within its frames: a marriage between my husband and myself as I imagined us, similarly aged, long into the future, with the joy of being at the table that afternoon with the two boys. It was the only tribute I could pay that felt honest to all parties, while remaining privately coded; a clue only for those who needed to know. I shot the food from above so that each dish filled the frame; veal and risotto oozing; the intensely wrinkled skin of the long-baked pears. The camera stayed on the couple's hands as they passed dishes back and forth, a sharing menu filled with touch. Hands grasping fancy cutlery, which they fingered tenta- tively before the demands of their appetites took over: steak knives to tear through meat, and curved spoons to drink soup from. Only as the meal continued did the camera pull out, enabling you to see their setting within a corner of a busy hotel dining room, and both the concentration and the pleasure on their faces. The marriage would later be crushed by the weight of inheritance and filial greed, but for now, there was only the purity of intention and unfiltered optimism. I was lucky that I could still share meals like that with my husband, for in committing to him came a vow of simplicity: we would enjoy what we had and what was there, for it had been long fought for and earned. The boys were still far from that, and as we sat in the hotel suite I was unable to ascertain their future. I felt invested but it was not my business. There were only wishes and fears, which I buried with smiles and congratulations. This was the way of all parents who understood that their children needed to make their own way, however hazardous. Take me to that mural later, Lorien said to Tom. If it's closed off like you say then we can have the place to ourselves. We'll have some time before we need to get ready for the premiere. Tom glowed with the feeling of being wanted, and of his point of view being necessary to another. He was no longer the student, but a man of his own standing who had knowledge to share. Sure, he said, if you like. The photos I took don't really do it justice. I want to see what you see, said Lorien simply. Feel it the way you do. And that was how it was left. We finished our meal, carrying out our threat to clear the dessert from the table, and after a cigarette on the terrace, softly rolled to our respective suites to continue our round of interviews. I watched them as they walked the corridor ahead of me, Lorien pulling Tom close; both content with their declarations and of the world that gave them the freedom to express that. A world outside of Hollywood; once back there who knew which resolutions they'd allow to fade, passing off their light-headedness as a European idyll which could not translate? In thinking of freedoms, I imagined Cosima walking the same corridor arm in arm with the man who'd defined her, and afterwards, stalking the hallways alone as she left gifts and notes for her phantom neighbour. I thought of Tom in the same position, and again, with a similarly obsessed Lorien. The story was a gift in that it could be pulled in so many ways, while still fulfilling the spirit of the person who wrote it. Lorien was right in his comment that we led a deferred life. All I wanted was to run to my room and sketch these ideas over the afternoon, but the interviews were waiting, making my imagined life secondary to the false one of sitting before the cameras. In the interview suite, I asked the publicist for ten minutes alone, enabling me to scribble those thoughts I feared would leave me before the end of the afternoon; less to do with dream-catching, more a preservation of mood. I was filled with hope after our lunch and wanted to find a way to carry that on to the film. I could write and film despair and helplessness without similar effort, for it was easy for the unhappiness in my past to rise to the surface, so often was it referred to and used – whether through dialogue, action or a lighting tone I wanted to replicate. Uncensored hope required work, and this was what I marked down in those precious few minutes to myself: a pathway which would help to guide me through the visual language of the film. I pushed myself to get down as much as I could, hoping that ten minutes could be extended to fifteen, willing my hand to keep up to speed with my volley of thoughts. When writing morphs into an out-of-body experience where space and time no longer matter, and you are only aware of the harmony of transcribing your thoughts with the scratch of the pen across the page, it can be something close to music. Ten minutes was all I needed to draw the architecture for the film. I had two sheets of hotel notepaper in my hand, which I folded with care before slipping them inside my jacket pocket. I felt them flat against my chest; the weight of lumber and dreams; bricks and masonry dragged into place by a crew of fifty. It felt like the equivalent of writing a pop song in a heartbeat: I was as giddy. I had meat and bones, and suddenly I could breathe. I had lived through a month of airlessness and only now was I truly aware of that; the power of my hand as I wrote, marvelling at its ability to divine; making sense of all that had puzzled me into two coherent pages which could make the film. Finally, at last, I had something concrete in my hands.

9.

I slept for over an hour following the afternoon's work, physically aching from the effort of speaking my mind. The first interview was together with Gabi where we talked about the business of film, and the challenges of adapting *The Folded Leaf* for the screen, financially and otherwise. I was then left alone for three further interviews in which I talked about my wider filmography in greater detail. Before Gabi left, I told her about Cosima's novel and my intention to film it, to which she did not act surprised. When you asked for those books yesterday, you had that look you get, she said, when something's brewing. Now we know what that brew is. I had the book sent down to her room so that she could read it before the premiere. We're here for another few days, I said, so it's imperative that we have an agreement to buy the film rights before we leave, especially as both the publisher and author are based here. I have a feeling we may have to pay well for them, but I can live with the expense.

Anxiety made me a spendthrift, knowing that I would pay whatever amount was asked. It would be for Gabi to barter them down afterwards. Only when she left to look at the book and start making calls did I relax. Junkets served to put you on a war footing: you ran on adrenalin and a fear steeped in your guts. In my younger days that fear came from being seen as an imposter; a man who filled film stock with scenes which were essentially blank, of promising moments here and there which did not successfully cohere into a film. I also wanted to be seen as a usurper, and played up to that role, with rock-star sunglasses and a detached air. But that was before I understood that I was not in combat, instead being given an opportunity to explain myself; to sell both the film and my aesthetic ideas behind it. I lost the vanity of the sunglasses for a greater egotism, that I was a thinker who was listened to. The knowledge of that ruined me also for a couple of years, until I calmed down and simply spoke of how I felt at the time: if I was happy with the outcome of the film, I showed it; if the repression in the wider culture angered me, I would give them that also. What allowed me to keep coming back was that the films were mostly good, and they were loved, giving something of the world, which allowed forgiveness of my youthful arrogance. It felt as if I had talked endlessly that afternoon, both of the film and to Lorien and Tom, and now my head pounded from the strain of counsel. It fizzed also, from the accomplishment of drafting the treatment for the next film. Something of that had given me additional energy to get through the afternoon. I

felt high because of it, giddy as I climbed the stairs to my
room. It had taken effort not to grin through the interviews,
the happiness that flooded me as those sheets of hotel notepaper prodded my chest. It allowed me space to breathe
should *The Folded Leaf* be loathed that evening – but I no
longer believed that it would, for the reactions to the pre-
views had been so overwhelming. It meant I spoke
unguardedly about the challenge of transposing Maxwell's
novel to Italy, and why I had thought it necessary. I chan-
nelled a little of the boys' breeziness, saying that ageing the
actors a couple of years out of a school setting, and into the
life of itinerant farm hands, was the only way I could see the
story working as a film, and that either you would understand that or the film wasn't for you. I was back to the cocky
twenty-five-year-old who had nothing to lose: take it or
leave it; only with it now came the humility of age, that I
recognised my limitations as a human being. My world view
is unlikely to change, I said to one journalist. I always want
to learn more, but my beliefs in freedoms and challenging
societal strictures will not lessen over time. If anything, I
feel greater anger now than I did even a decade ago. What
I cannot change is my eye and the way that I see the world.
It's a viewpoint or curiosity that shapes all my films, includ-
ing this one. But each film is so different, the interviewer
said, moving centuries and continents. You shouldn't get
caught up in all that, I said. That comes from passion and
the desire to move forward, but where the movies are set is
essentially window dressing; the illusion of cinema. Look

behind that to deconstruct the stories they tell. They all exist
on the same spectrum, each connected to the other. I slept
because of the weight of paper wedged in my pocket, and
because Tom had taken Lorien to see the mural. Their interviews finished half an hour before mine and I heard their
laughter as they escaped the confines of the suite. The walled
garden would become their place now; the mural itself a
signifier of what they shared. There was a place for me
within that, but this was not how it would primarily be
known. It's remarkable what you can come to terms with in
a short space of time. Cosima's mural had become theirs, to
which I would have limited visiting rights, and I didn't feel
as wounded as I'd anticipated. I rang my husband on waking.
How are you feeling? he asked. Good, I said. Almost excited,
if you can believe that. I can, he said, you sound much
lighter than yesterday. What happened? I told him about
how well the interviews were going, and the boys' success
in charming everyone. You'd love it if you were here, I said.
It's frantic, but there's calm on the horizon. I don't believe
that for a second, he laughed. Do your job and enjoy it.
We're home waiting for you. He would never attend another
festival, at least while our boy was still at school, packing me
off with a pep talk and a kiss. You're a genius, and this is the
only time I'll flatter you by saying that. Go mingle with
those other genii, but know that you'll outshine them all.
Be as selfish as you want. Fall back into your bad habits if
you need to. Whatever gives you the confidence to get
through it. If a trophy is yours for the taking, grab it from

the jury's hands. Screw those youngsters who think they know better. What I most wanted to share with him was my ideas on the next film, but that could not happen without an argument, and I could not attend the premiere with the carcase of a row rotting inside me. Instead, he gave a revised version of his pep talk, and handed the phone to our boy, just returned from school, who needed my interest in his football score more than anything to do with film. Directors who travelled with their families did not make them closer; they were just more likely to argue at close quarters. The honesty of our arrangement worked precisely because I was the least important person in my household, and that made me happy. Heart full, I rang Cosima. Just checking that you're not bailing out on tonight, I said. I've asked that you sit with me and my editor. We'll be in the front row. Why would you do that? she said. I'm nobody. You're our guest, I said. That makes you a person of interest. Also, there might be photographers, just to warn you. I'd rather be hidden in one of the back rows, she said. I prefer an aisle seat so that I can leave quickly if I need to. A crowded cinema makes me anxious. I usually avoid them for this reason. Whatever makes you comfortable, I said, but just so you know, there is no crowding in the front row. She laughed. I'm not what you call arm candy, if that's what you're looking for in your photographs. I'm not looking for arm candy, I said, just a friend who might be interested in seeing the new film. I should tell you that I haven't seen your last three films, she said. It's easier to be clear now than dance around it later.

You've missed nothing, I said. All rubbish. This one's probably no better. That's cute, she said, but you're too old for modesty. I'll be there, don't worry. My editor, Stjepan, arrived and we went to smoke in the garden. Of all my collaborators, he was the one to lead me into bad habits. During dark periods in the edit suite when nothing seemed to gel – there were usually two or three days like that in every film we'd cut together – he'd take me a dive bar and get me drunk. Piss those neuroses away, maestro, he'd say. Piece this film together with new eyes. He didn't look at me with the same expression now. This wasn't what I was expecting, maestro, he said. You're never hysterical, but there's always a show of nerves in one way or another. Either you talk incessantly or you don't talk at all. Sometimes you disappear for a couple of hours. But no, here you are at the appointed time, and I've never seen you so calm. It's almost like you know something. I'm as blind as you are, I said. I'm ready for the film to be seen, and I stand by it. Even when we were taking about a potential edit this morning, he said, I had the feeling that your heart wasn't in it. Like, we were discussing the possibility because we always discussed the possibility. It's a touchstone of these festivals. Almost like a lucky charm. But you barely scratched the surface of what we could do, which tells me we aren't going to touch it. We're not, I said. I'm as sure as I can be. I knew it, he said, clapping his hands. It was on my mind the whole flight over. Half preparing myself for three days of hunkering down. I mean, everything's ready if you need it, but I thought, That's not the tone of a man who's changing his mind. You sounded distracted, so our ritual felt more like a gesture. Like when you pass a church and you touch your hand against the door out of some latent deference or respect, but you don't know why you're doing it. I mean, we never change anything, but this time it felt like you weren't even trying to persuade yourself. You know the film, I said. It's perfect as it is. It's better than perfect, he said, but you're too modest to say it. I don't think we've made better work. Everything we learned from all the other films has been rolled into this one. So you're saying it's a copy, I joked. Aha, he said, I'm not falling for that one! You had to make this film. Only you could've made this film. And you got it right, that's the beauty of it. The boys got it right, I corrected. The boys! he said. They're going to be like gods when everyone gets to see it. Have you told them how their lives will change? Lorien already knows, I can see it, I said. Tom's ready for the outcome. It's what he's been waiting for his whole life, but whether he's actually prepared to hear those words from me or anyone close to him, I don't know. We hugged, our cigarettes still hanging from the corner of our mouths. Rock 'n' roll, he laughed, a cigarette burn from kissing you on the neck. I'm glad you made it, I said. It wouldn't be the same without you here. Where else would I be? he said, gesturing around the garden. This is my family. The garden suite remained ours, and I asked everyone to join me for a drink before we left for the screening. Gabrijela was already out on the terrace, pouring champagne. If no one's joining me, I'm going to finish this bottle by myself, she said. I've rung the boys twice and they seem to have disappeared. They'll be along, I said. In the meantime, I'll take a couple of glasses. How are you feeling? she asked. Ready, I said. Once the film runs it becomes truly real, and I want it to be real. Look at him, joked Stjepan, he's calmer than both of us. How did that happen? I think he meditates, said Gabi. Either that or he's found God. In which case, I need to find a new director, he laughed, because I didn't sign up for that. The company was staffed with heretics, a rejection of our collective pasts which had held us together over the decades. We stood in the quiet of the garden and celebrated our kinship: through a combination of hard work, respect and good health we had a finished film in our hands. I was emotional and proud, knowing I would be nothing without those around me. I did not believe in luck, but there was a blessing to be said for the serendipity that had brought these people into my world: Gabi moving into the dorm room next to mine on our first day at film school; meeting Stjepan at a rock gig in Zagreb shortly after I graduated, where he was piecing together Super 8 projections between apprenticing at the city's cutting rooms. The three of us had stood in many gardens like this one, toasting success or disaster. We'd fought, cried and celebrated our work together for over thirty years. We knew each other's tics and vanities, speaking a language that only came from the shared experience of working on our films. Is there any music? I asked. There's supposed to be a stereo connected somewhere.

Put your phone on the deck, said Gabi. It'll play whatever you want. We blasted out Siouxsie and the Banshees, because we wouldn't have got together without punk. The three of us now, still in our black and leather, moshing in the court-yard garden with the same intent as we did at the gigs that moved us all those years ago. Our dance was customary before the official screening; something tribal in our think-ing which had never left. Dancing unified us and made us stronger to face the world. We would celebrate further afterwards, but this moment remained an important one, another touchstone that we could not live without. We managed two full songs before stabilising ourselves; our chests pumping and blood rising to our faces. That's just what I needed, for my make-up to run into my dress, Gabi complained, but she was happy for it, cementing as it did our love and union. We each had another glass, which made me light-headed, having not eaten since lunchtime. I was enjoy-ing being carefree with my family, almost as if it wasn't my film at all, but that of a contemporary that I had a passing interest in. I knew that I would feel something stronger once we left the palazzo; there was a moment in a theatre as the lights went down that you truly understood the depth of your vulnerability: that for all the good wishes and the boosting presence of family around you, the truth that you were about to be judged was inescapable. Your visual imagination and use of language, your depth and humour, as well as compassion and emotional intelligence: these were to be dissected, held aloft and appraised. I knew of no other art form that took apart a human being to the same degree of complexity, aside from perhaps singers. Performers were given a wider canvas on which to fail because of the degree of wish fulfilment that went with their role; what you projected on to a singer or band was so intensely personal; how to critique a singer's performance was in some way to also critique your own biography, for the two were permanently intertwined. Film was different for the screen itself was the point of separation between you and the viewer. For this reason, it could be crueller and cut deeper. I was being truthful in what I'd said: I was happy and excited, but the feeling that I was dancing before a forthcoming execution remained. What have we here, called a voice from the doorway, the maestro throwing a sneaky party? Lorien, slick and suited, grinned as he walked in, Tom and our publicist close behind. It was something to do with the falling spring light, and the warmth we were feeling from three champagne cocktails, but the arrival of the boys took our breath away. They looked perfect and magic, both in black, so becoming part of us, yet other than, at the same time: Lorien in a close-fitting suit; Tom more bohemian in a shorter suit, with a leather jacket embossed with black graffiti. Not too shabby, right? asked Tom, recognising the looks on our faces as something he had seen before and had successfully dealt with. They were already on pedestals waiting to be adored. Their function for the evening was to be idolised by everyone they touched, and their preparation showed in the energy by which they entered the room. I thought of their elevator journey down, when this mode had switched on, whether separately or transmitted through a kiss or a shared glance. Either way, we were drinking with movie stars – they were still family but for now, we were cowed by their elevation. I'll take a drink for Lorien, but I'm fine with water, said Tom. We've a lot of talking to do tonight and I don't want to jumble my words. Afterwards, you can throw as many drinks down my neck as you like, but I want to do you proud when we're called to speak about the film. I'm counting on it, said Lorien, with a smile. I want to get you so drunk you won't know which country you're in. You need to experience that at least once. I don't need to hear any of that! said the publicist, covering her ears. When we were at a distance from the others I asked Lorien what he thought of the painting. The building's a dump, he said. Looks even worse in daylight. As for the painting itself, I get that it's probably a masterpiece of its kind, but it didn't do anything for me at first. The longer I looked at it, the colder I felt. Couldn't work out whether that was down to his failure as an artist – like, it was missing one crucial element which would make it pop – or whether it was down to what I lack as a spectator. But … there was presence there. Something unexplained that ran through me like an electric shock. Like, I was registering this guy's life force, his determination, even if I wasn't truly in love with the piece. It was at that point that I started to turn. You see, I said, it's undeniable! Quite, he said, but helped also by looking at Tom. He was so absorbed within it. The wonder on his face took my breath away. You have a similar expression whenever it's mentioned. Both these things made me realise its value. What will you do with that? I asked. It's more what I've done, he said, grinning again. I'm buying it. As a surprise for Tom. The whole apartment building for us to use if that's what he wants. The caretaker told me what one of the owners tried asking for it last year before the wider family objected. It's not cheap, but it's still peanuts if you look at what they paid me for my last film. Money does nothing just sitting there, so I'm asking my business manager to look into it. You're buying it as a gift? I said, holding down the emotion I felt. For me as much as him, Lorien said. He wants a place here and now so do I. I thought I was an Angeleno for ever, but I'm learning that you can change your mind in a heartbeat if you meet someone worthwhile. Whether the four storeys can be converted into something we can actually use, I don't know, and don't even care about right now. It's more symbolic, of me and Tom having our hand in something, together. I nodded my agreement that I would keep the news to myself until the deal was accepted. These two are at it again, called the publicist, approaching us. Art, art, art. As if there aren't more important things to be talking about. Italy is art and food, I said. We have nothing else to discuss. Aside from this incredible film we've made, said Tom quickly. It's been strange talking about something that I still haven't seen yet. The journalists didn't know that, obviously, but it felt a little like they knew a secret that we didn't. Now we're about to find out what the fuss is all about.

The publicist looked appalled, but I had to stifle something building in my chest on seeing how fast he had come to Lorien's aid; his instinct to protect now fine-tuned and efficient. Oh my God, said the publicist, lapsing into a defensive barrage of how all the select press who'd attended the preview had been briefed thoroughly, and that if Tom hadn't paid attention to the DVD screener she'd left in his room, that was out of her control. There's only so much I can do, she said, holding her arms aloft. These are hands, not wands. Relax, laughed Tom. I'm only yanking your chain. I made a clear decision not to see any more of the film past the rough cut until tonight. Maestro knows why. Too much of what we do is orchestrated. Removes the element of surprise. I hate to break it to you, but you acted in that movie, said Gabi, so you know how it ends, to which Lorien clapped his hands and broke into laughter. That's not what I'm saying, continued Tom. What I want is a sense of expectation when I slide down into my seat. There'll be something that I haven't seen that made the finished cut, I guarantee it. I want to be enveloped. To feel what I felt when we made the film. That only comes from stepping back into the unknown. It was the strongest argument he had given and everyone in the room was taken by the force of it, our publicist physically stepping back as the impact of his words took hold. And that's not a sound bite we're going to use in any interviews either, he grinned, reaching over to give her a hug. Just something between us. If it helps, the only reason I haven't seen the finished film is because I think it's going to be

terrible, said Lorien, immediately lifting the room, and protecting his boy the way that he'd been protected. Let's drink
to that, I said, raising my glass. To a terrible film! A disaster!
everyone agreed. It was only our euphoria that could've led
us down this path. If I'd attempted the same at previous
festivals, the actors would have openly revolted, no matter
their confidence. Tom and Lorien inspired an irreverence
underpinned by the strength of their performances in the
film. It was the scope of their talent, their innate understanding of it, which allowed them to speak in such an offhand
way, coupled with the security of speaking to the heart of
the family. I thought of my son, who was still at the age
where sitting through one of my films or handling one of
my husband's books held no interest. It looks boring, Dad,
he said. Why can't you make cartoons? I imagined him ten
years from now, God willing, accompanying me to a similar
festival and making the same comment, only this time stemming from pride in my work rather than disinterest. I longed
for the day when I would see that pride on his face. Our
publicist responded to her beeping phone. The cars are outside, she said, and the mood changed once again, as we
prepared to do the jobs expected of us. I was to take the first
car with Gabi and Stjepan, with Lorien and Tom following
behind. They need to make an entrance, the publicist
explained. Once they arrive, everyone else will get ignored.
That's why I want to get your pictures out of the way first.
Hear that? joked Gabi. We're getting a minute of spotlight
before we have to hand it back. But everything had been

planned in great detail in advance, so that none of this was a surprise to us; we simply remained in a rebellious mood. Our publicist went on ahead, leaving us to finish the final round of champagne, but we were more subdued now. Lorien and Tom perched on the sofa arms, talking between themselves and taking pictures of each other for their social media, wanting to conserve their energy for when it was needed most. They were probably running at forty per cent, but still they shone. I'm not going to do any interviews on my own, I said to the others. I've had my fill of being locked away. So if there's any talking to be done, let's do it as the three of us, yes? Well, they got me these fancy trousers to go with my leather jacket, so I might as well make the most of it, said Stjepan. Just get them to point the camera and mic in my direction and I'll speak until they scream blue murder. You don't have to go that far, said Gabi. We'll just throw the answers back and forth between each other. A little like a kid's game, I said. Stjepan laughed. There speaks a man with a child under ten! The procession as we headed for the cars; the bow of the concierge, and the best wishes of another hotel guest who passed us in the corridor. We were now in the midst of ceremony, which could not be altered or escaped from. For all the despised monarchies scattered across the continent, a love of ceremony remained. We were nothing but serfs, but there was still gravitas in our glide and steps, feeling the power of the moment. This was the point during younger days when I let it go to my head, exaggerating my regal credentials within cinema: the foundling child who was actually a crown prince. I had no truck with that nonsense now, but to reject ceremony was to insult those who still respected it, so I shook the concierge's hand as he wished me luck, and acknowledged the greeting of the woman we passed in the corridor. The worst could not happen if you were surrounded by positive forces; every comment and gesture passed in our direction as we left the palazzo feeling akin to swords or shields being held aloft by our protectors. This carried though to our arrival at the festival cinema and a further photo call on the red carpet against their branded backdrop. The publicist was right in that the photographers' interest in us lasted no more than a couple of minutes, our tired flesh no competition for the main event to follow. But the energy and heat were undeniable; the noise and buzz, allowing us to momentarily feel that we were not just at the centre of something, but that we were the centre from which the night radiated. We were rock stars for two minutes and I'd forgotten the thrill of that, fleeting but wanted. There was love and good wishes from those calling out my name, which made me grateful; Gabi and Stjepan enjoyed it as much as me, the latter pulling faces once he tired of playing it straight. Outside the cinema, there was a crowd of spectators on the sidewalk, separated from the red carpet by a line of crash barriers, overseen by patrolling security. I thought back to my youth when my obsession with movies began. If I lived in a festival city, would I have stood against the crash barriers as these mostly young people were, hoping that if I did so, something of film's magic or inspiration would wash over me as actors, directors and screenwriters walked by? Either that or some free tickets. If I lived nowhere near such a town, would I feel the urge to travel there, the way other kids crossed country for a gig? How far would I have gone in pursuit of stardust if such apparatus had been available to me? There had to be kids now who saw through the mirage of flashbulbs and stars, but was there a place for them to observe what happened on the red carpet in order to utilise the experience later, or were they at home finding an alternative route to their future? I knew that if I was sixteen years old I would be fighting my way to the front of the barrier. Dreams were one thing, but the buzz was more addictive; the whip and fury of activity pulling an introspective boy out of his head and bringing him down to the realities of the premiere: photographers who shouted insults and were aggressive in other ways in order to get their picture; television reporters cutting ahead of their rivals to get their scoop, running around and past each other as if in a playground; starlets limping in too tight shoes, or speaking breathlessly because of dresses that pulled severely across their ribcage; the cocksure strut of diminutive actors, convinced they were taller. And still through that, the excitement of seeing another world or being in the same breathing space as those you admired. I thought of how I'd react if I'd ever seen Bertolucci from the crash barriers or Anouk Aimée and Alain Delon, and how those feelings would manifest themselves. Was it just the notion of presence that ultimately seduced us, something that snuck past the intellect and instead attacked the heart and loins? What was it that pulled you out of your daydream and made you scream at your loudest? My questions answered in waves, as a series of roars from outside filled the lobby, indicating that Tom and Lorien had arrived, and jolting me back into the present.

10.

Cosima waited for us in a corner of the lobby. Her posture showed no signs of nerves, her feet at equal distance apart, planted firmly in her spot as if she owned the space, similar to how I'd first seen her outside the coffee bar. Her expression was one of detached amusement, making it clear to all who passed that she was outside the circus; possibly party to its secrets, but in no way believing of them. She projected an interest in cinema, and of areas outside of that; most strikingly in the cut of her black suit, chic and of the city, her hair pulled back from her face, showing the tendons in her neck and the milky skin there. She dressed too carefully to be a person who lived and breathed film, for she was neither sleepless nor ravaged. She belonged there while at the same time appearing to be slightly above its absurdity; only her eyes gave her away, as she scanned the doorway for a familiar face. I cut through the line of television cameras waiting to speak to us in order to greet her, kissing her cheeks for the first time. You made it, I said. I thought about not coming, she replied, but I'm no coward. I have a penultimate round of obligations before I can reclaim the evening, I said, gesturing towards the cameras. Do you want to wait for us in the bar? I'll stay here for a little while, she said with a smile. This is all new to me, so it'll be interesting to see you at work. I rejoined Gabrijela and Stjepan, sharing our responses back and forth as the questions came our way. I greeted the television journalists warmly, embracing those I'd known and who'd supported my work for years. You could not make films now if you were unable to answer questions from those who felt they had shares in you. There needed to be transparency in every frame shot, requiring you to be clear in what you wanted to remain secret or opaque. This spoon-feeding needled me, understanding that an increase in these opportunities lead to a greater discourse and exposure to the film, but were those taking part in the conversation drawing their own conclusions or merely amplifying what these journalists had told them to think? As a younger man who believed in making challenging films, I would push hard against this party line, filled with hatred for the finality of their judgements. What gave them the right to decree on a film after one-hundred-and-nineteen minutes what had taken me three years to perfect? But it was only the two hours that made the screen that mattered, your choices and sacrifices behind that meant nothing; your exhaustion and debt, pleasure and frustration were invisible to their eyes. All they saw and wanted to see

were the images that ran through the projector. Criticism
was an art if you allowed it to be, and I now finally accepted
that church. So the official premiere screening for *The Folded
Leaf* is taking place tonight, and advance word from the few
lucky enough to see an advance run are talking of it as a
masterpiece in a career of masterpieces, began one reporter.
How do you feel about that? It's flattering, but I only think
of it in chronological terms, I said. It's my latest film, and
that's it. I don't spend time reflecting on what I've done
before, except when I'm asked in situations like this. But you
agree that it's a masterpiece? he persisted. That's not for me
to say, I replied. What the jury and others take from the film
is out of my hands. I only care about the present moment,
and possibly the one after that. Don't let him fool you, said
Gabi. He's thrilled at the responses. We all are. Would you
say that this is a personal work, maestro? Your parents met
working on a farm. You spent your early years in the countryside. Is this a love letter to your youth? All my films are
love letters, I said. Even the angry ones. No, the greatest debt
the film owes is to William Maxwell and his novel, *The
Folded Leaf.* Without that book, we wouldn't have a film.
And what in that book spoke to you, or convinced you to
adapt it for the screen? You haven't worked from another
writer's source material for over a decade. Why now?
Maxwell understood the tension and pain of the unrequited.
I hadn't read him for many years, but my husband put the
novel in front of me after a discussion we'd had on the subject. As soon as I read it again, I knew that I wanted to film

it in some way. It was a very strong feeling. What was your thinking in casting for the lead roles? another asked. You're using actors you've never worked with before. What do Lorien and Tom bring to the characters of Spud and Lymie, aside from their star power? You can hear what they bring, I shouted through the roar still coming from outside. Electricity, passion, and an ability to totally give themselves up to the camera and the truth of their characters. We shot the film here last summer, a couple of hours from Genoa, but it wasn't a holiday for anyone. They pushed themselves incredibly hard, way out of their comfort zone, and you see that in the resulting film. And I'm sure it doesn't hurt to have their names on the poster, right, maestro? Lorien, especially, breaking out in his recent slew of roles. You misunderstand me, I said. I never care about who is and isn't a star, and all the calculations that come with that. All I care about is find-ing the right actors for the roles. These were the right guys. One last question, maestro: if you win the jury prize this year, you'll be the only filmmaker who's been awarded the trophy three times. How would that feel? Ask me tomorrow when they announce their choices, I said. For now, I hope that people enjoy the film and take something from it. That's as much as I can hope for as a filmmaker. You're really in charge, aren't you? said Cosima, when I joined her in the bar afterwards. I got to watch for a while before they moved me along. It was impressive. I'd feel swamped by those cameras, distracted by the noise, questions coming from corners, but you really own it. You're not fazed at all. I'm used to it, I said. The noise tonight is more raucous than I'm used to, but it's strangely energising. They need me to talk about the film and not be a wallflower, so you have to leave that side of you behind. I'm not sure if I could, said Cosima. When I was interviewed for the novel I had to talk to one journalist sitting side by side rather than across from each other, so that I wouldn't have to look into his face as I spoke. I think I insisted we go to a park and conduct the interview from a bench just so I'd feel comfortable. Are you comfortable now? I asked. I am after this drink, she laughed. It's not my event, so nothing's on me. You're in great spirits, I have to say, maestro. I thought you'd be a wreck. You cling on when you're in the midst of a whirlwind, I said, otherwise you fall. The bar was on the first floor with two balconies overlooking the crowd below. We smoked a cigarette and watched Tom and Lorien take pictures and sign autographs for the crowd. They'd been out there for half an hour and had still not tired of it, chatting and posing with everyone who asked. The time we spent making the film had been true in the sense that they'd shown themselves, but this side of them was true also: how they fed off the attention and seemed to grow from it, Tom rising in stature to reach Lorien's heights, in sync as they covered opposite ends of the barrier line to meet in the middle where the TV cameras were waiting. I longed for them to look up, even for a second, just so I could catch their eyes, but they were too engrossed in what was happening immediately around them. It was work, but also something more ethereal, a state which they still lacked the tools to define. This is the dream, isn't it? said Cosima. Young actors with all these kids at their feet. How do they navigate this and stay sane? By believing that they're not worthy of it, is how I wanted to answer, but I held back because I wanted to protect the boys. I knew that I could trust Cosima, but the nature of the boys' vulnerability was precious and in a small way kept me connected with them. Once that was shared, the thread would twist and fray, before breaking irrevocably. I watched them standing there with Lorien's arm draped around Tom's neck, before holding him close across the shoulder; vulnerability and strength in one photograph should they choose to see it. The reporters present did not have that second sight, too blinded by the promise and virility of young Hollywood at close quarters. It was left to the fans to dream, and to see the positioning of Lorien's arm as a clue to follow, but only because their yearning was greater; their fantasy being a purity of love, untouched by commerce. Cosima went to fetch more drinks, and I continued to gaze down at their gesture, until the publicist called me away. We took our seats in the front row and waited for the room to be filled. I kissed and shook hands with the members of the jury, a couple I was friendly with, the others new to me. The camaraderie among directors is different to that with actors, carrying less weight because of our competitive natures, unwilling to share our secrets. I had long thought that this was the same with novelists, also: that if you were lucky, you'd find a group of brothers and sisters who had your back and would possibly defend your creative life – as you would theirs, unthinkingly – but still without one hundred per cent trust, because you could never be sure whether the experience you shared with them would become material. So to hide this fact from ourselves, we subsequently saw very little of each other, aside from these occasions: at festivals or during the award season. There was always honesty in the way we hugged one another, indicating that we were family, despotic sufferers all, with our jealousies and inferiority complexes; so much to share, but always more comfortable at this distance. I promised you the front row, I said to Cosima, but there are also a couple of seats in the row behind if that makes you more comfortable. Aisle seats? she asked. Not quite, I said, but two seats down so you won't feel too closed in, hopefully. That sounds fine to me, she said. I'm nobody to make demands. You should be accommodating the whims of your actors or the jury friends rather than worry about me. I'm a multi-tasker, I smiled. This is how I make films. Where will you sit? she asked. In the seat directly in front of you, I said. If you don't like the film, you can give my chair a kick. I'll hiss, she said. It's less ambiguous. Gabi and Stjepan joined us on the bottom steps, where I made some introductions. Ah, Cosima, Gabi said, kissing her warmly on both cheeks, I'm reading your novel at the moment. You are? she asked. I started it this afternoon. It's heartbreaking, and brilliant. What talent you have! Any woman who's been broken, that's to say all of us, will recognise something of themselves in it. Gabi looked at me as she finished speaking, as if to deliver her appraisal on the film's potential, but was then called away before she could expand further. You showed her the book? Cosima asked. You know how much I'm taken with it, I replied. And when I feel something to that degree, I want to share it with my team. It'll pass into Stjepan's hands here, just as soon as Gabi's finished it. He loads us up with materials, said Stjepan. Books and films. He has taste, the old boy, so it's always needed, even if you don't appreciate it at the time. Do you mind it being shared, Cosima? I asked, noticing how pale she had become and that she would no longer meet my eye. I have nothing to complain about, she said. Books are there to be read, even forgotten ones. It just takes some getting used to. The room was filling at a faster rate now, and we took our seats. Tom and Lorien would be the last to arrive, entering once the lights dimmed. Typically I would have done the same, but I wanted to dispel the mystery of the room by studying the faces that would be judging me, no different to a stage actor peeping through the curtains before a performance. Only I was less coy about it. I wanted them to register my face as I met theirs; to make eye contact and get their measure, whether friend or foe. It was one last confrontation before battle, and I used whatever stature I had to my best advantage, so that they could see me under the full house lights and be reminded of who I was. It was wicked of me to relish that moment but I did, not knowing when it would happen again. Stjepan gestured towards my seat. Sit down, maestro, and stop grinning at everyone. You look like a lunatic. I'm happy, I said, nodding towards the audience. I know that, he said, but let's not frighten the animals before the film starts. I see you, psyching them out. OK, I laughed, I'm sitting, I'm sitting, patting him on the shoulder as I took my place. Did you see the boys? I asked. They were walking them to one of the offices to wait there, he said. I think they were still taking photographs with people as they cut through the bar. Everyone wants to see them. That's because they're movie stars, I said, even at this festival, they're like rare beasts. That combination of charisma with the promise of their careers about to open up. It's the romance of being on the cusp of greatness. Of promise fulfilled. You're aware that the process is starting, but don't yet know how it will end. That's where the hysteria lies, in a space between the present and the future, and all based on wishes, longing and dreams. It's the present that never ceases to amaze me, he said. When you see them around set, they're these shy things with spots and greasy hair, more comfortable with blending into the background, and then once it's all over, they become larger than life. Lorien and Tom are neither, I said. They're still the boys we know. But I was lying to myself, for I was further removed from their shifting reality with every picture they took. Every camera phone shot was a further brick built into their guard. It was for me to understand which side of the wall I would find myself on once the film had run. The three seats to my right remained empty, belonging to the boys and Gabi. By this point the room was full and the chatter switched to a lower, more expectant tone. This was the final screening of the day, so there was pooling of latent energy, unspent from hours of sitting in the dark. My stomach was knotted, now filled with acid that slowly rose up my throat. A rigorous burn accompanied that rise, penetrating through tissue and attacking my blood. I knew it was the result of too much champagne on an empty stomach, but it felt like the sign of a greater impediment, my body recognising something that my mind could not yet accept; that I was sitting with more enemies than friends, and how I was still capable of foolish thoughts and committing that to the screen. How I was an imposter in a room full of them, but somehow greater, for the willingness to deny my failures in believing that I'd made something good. The festival director would shortly address the audience and the anxiety I felt in that moment overtook all other rationalities. It was as acute a state as I'd experienced for some time, believing the room to be slowly decompressing, my body overheating and fighting for breath. In everything I'd felt in the days leading up to the screening, the one state I'd dismissed was blind panic, because I was not the same man as before, overworked and disabled by sadness. My life was rich and I had people around me who anticipated the warning signs before they were apparent even to me, ensuring that I rested, or that my mind and body were occupied with something other than film, whether that was a game of softball in the park with my family or driving up the coast to discover a new restaurant. Through them and my own strength of mind, I was able to avoid these holes, but the swell of utter helplessness took me by surprise. I was rooted to my seat, paralysed, unable to communicate to Stjepan what was happening. He was engrossed in conversation with Cosima, turning around to face her; his back, a wall. I struggled for no more than a minute, but an epoch had flashed by in that time. It was Gabi who would draw me out, appearing as she did with some urgency. You need to come upstairs, now, she said. There's some trouble with Tom and he won't come down. All my thoughts went to him, pushing myself up from my seat and quickly following her. As I passed Cosima I fleetingly remembered my comment to her that morning on the body protecting itself when the mind was too consumed, and here was my physical approximation of that. Tom cut a restless figure as he paced the emptiness of the bar, Lorien standing by a sofa away from the window but watching him closely. I can't go in there, he said on seeing me. His eyes were still wide from the high of earlier, and the noise from the crowd still waiting outside, but behind that lay the recognition of the moment to come, facing his intimate performance in a room filled with strangers. When I first signed up with my agent, he warned me about getting into poorly thought-out situations, he said. This feels like one of those. In what way? I asked. He warned me never to see myself on screen for the first time in a place that wasn't safe, Tom said. He'd had actors who fucked themselves up by watching the film they made in the wrong environment. Watch it wherever it's going to make you happy, I said. Maybe with other films I could sit there and be a good sport, but with this one I don't think I can, he said. It means too much. I want to totally surrender in watching the film. To give myself in the way we did when we made it, but if I sit in there, I can't let it show on my face, and that kills me. No one's going to make you do anything you don't want to, said Lorien, rubbing his back, as if it were the knots in his body at the root of the disruption. Don't pat me like I'm a fucking baby, said Tom, shaking him off to continue his striding. I'm not a baby, so don't treat me like one. Let me work it out for myself. Lorien moved back but did not rise, simply holding his gaze as he sat down. Whatever you need, dude, he said, nodding towards me. We're good with whatever you decide, I said. They're here to see the film, not to see the backs of your heads in the auditorium, said Gabi. You don't need to be there. Listen to what Gabi says, said Lorien. She has wisdom. In the scheme of things, being a no-show is not that big of a deal, said Gabi. It's fine. No one has to die, Tom, said Lorien. So chill. In response, Tom went and sat before him, the reduction of movement calming both. Might have been easier if you'd come to that conclusion earlier, Lorien continued, the tightness in his mouth relaxing. But that's OK. You call the shots. I didn't want you to be angry with me, Tom said, turning to me. Nodding to indicate that I felt nothing of the kind, I sat beside him, his face marked with the pale torment of youth, but still a determination that he could not be swayed. There was a helplessness to Lorien also, for all the comfort he gave, he too was learning how much to share of himself and what to protect. From a distance, now standing over Tom's seated figure on the sofa, he looked like a guardian, until he moved forward and rubbed his shoulders with the ease of a lover; once again using touch to lessen the situation, finding a way through his fingertips to calm and restore where more vocal reasoning had failed. I told him that it wasn't a big deal if we skipped the film, he said. It happens plenty of times. So long as we're hanging around for the Q&A afterwards, no one cares whether we're sitting in the room or not. I care, said Tom again, maybe too much. That's the problem. I understood then what he needed: to see the film while there remained a degree of adrenalin pumping through his veins, with only those he loved to support him. We can watch it in the projectionist's booth, I said. She'll be fine about it and you'll get the privacy you need. How does that sound? That works, said Gabi. Go there now, and I'll tell the festival president that he can make his speech. Once they roll the credits, I'll bring you down for the Q&A. We were parents to our collaborators, Gabi and I; the ability to solve problems being one of the key elements that bonded us, so long as we did not have to hone that skill on ourselves. Tom softened as the agitation of before left, knowing that in other instances, solutions would not be found so quickly because those around him either cared less or believed their needs to be greater. He would work on movies where his involvement was no greater than hitting his mark and delivering his lines convincingly. He would be adored on other film sets, but never to the same degree again because this was the first time all the disparate elements in the universe had aligned, and the feeling from that, its uniqueness, could never be replicated. Once that was clear, everything he did, in hindsight, would never be matched, even if he spent the rest of his career looking. Let's go, he said. Will she let me eat popcorn there? You can snack, said the projectionist when we arrived, but there's no booze in here. She pulled out two stools and pointed to a desk chair next to the table holding the stacked reels. Make yourselves comfortable. You'll get used to the noise. Once you learn to shut it out, you can see and hear everything they do in the house downstairs. Do you want to listen to what the festival director's saying? she asked, pointing towards the glass. I've muted the sound as the machines warm up. It's the only quiet you'll get for the next two hours, but let me know. I shook my head. We're happy with the peace, I said, pulling my chair towards the boys so that we now sat in a semicircle to the right of the projector, out of its glare, but with a fine vista through the glass and the screen beyond. Lorien's hand gripped Tom's knee to keep him still. Have you ever watched a film in a projection room? she asked the boys. I'm guessing not. Aside from believers like the maestro here, they all shoot on digital these days. This experience will be different, trust me. This is what cinema is: the noise, torn sprockets patched together; the heat, and smell of burning from the machine. This is the grunt work that gives them outside the magic they crave. How lucky you are to see both. She felt the tension of her guests and was doing her best to make things sweeter, for the experience inside the booth could be a mismatched one. You saw the same film as watched by those in the auditorium, but at a further remove because of the glass divider. It was not that the impact of image and sound were delayed, more that it felt as if you were about to watch an echo of what the film actually was. Whatever I had made would be reduced to an essence within this space, making the reality of spotting off-notes jarring and enlarged. But my interest piqued at the prospect, knowing that it was one further way to examine the film, and how I would enjoy conferring with Stjepan about it afterwards. The position was difficult for as much of my instinct was to be with the boys and to see the film as they saw it, to study them as much as the film, gauging their reactions and emotional responses, I was also drawn to sitting among strangers, to absorb the arc of their responses also, a methodology rooted in both science and masochism. I had sat in a full cinema for every film I'd made, needing to get my hands dirty after months of clinical precision in the editing room. I knew directors who produced one film after the next without ever engaging with their audience, believing their work to exist in a vacuum where there was no feedback or consequences. I did not have that arrogance, it was impossible to be imperious to that degree with my origins, coming from a country built on collectivism and potatoes, but nor did I explicitly chase approval of those who paid to see my work. My forays were more investigative than conversational: I would buy a ticket and enter the room once the lights dimmed and left before the credits rolled. I was not compelled to stay and chat afterwards, nor would I read the completed questionnaires that various distributors would foist upon Gabi and myself before the wider release of more difficult films, when they angled for a shorter edit. I was only after visceral confirmation that I had followed my instincts truthfully, and that only came from sitting among the audience as they laughed, cried, slept or talked between themselves over the parts they found confusing. For all my fears, I felt the weight of flesh and blood expectations in those public, out-of-town screenings in a way that I did not on set, making the experience a levelling one; giving a heightened awareness of what stirred the soul and what failed it. Lorien and Tom would be stirred by different things as they watched: their memory of shooting on a particular day; a location or prop they valued; the first touch of the other's hand setting an unknown counter-story into motion. They would see what I saw, but also fathoms that were out of my reach and could never be touched. As the titles ran, Lorien again gripped Tom's leg as if to anchor them – a familiar gesture that was becoming theirs, expected and wanted – before patting me on the shoulder. This is what we've been waiting for, maestro, he said. Let's see how you do. When I think about that screening now, it's the film's distilled essences that resonate most strongly over the flux of anxiety and admiration that had earlier disabled me. There was an image of Tom resting his head on Lorien's shoulder also, allowing himself to be vulnerable in front of a woman he'd never met but intuited was to be trusted after watching how I interacted with her. Once they were comfortable, pulling off their jackets and throwing them on to the table behind, Lorien kissed his forehead, keenly aware of what he was doing. His concern was for Tom, but at the same time testing the water of how far he could go; the festival trip a series of first steps, running towards a spark of fire and experiment that would continue to burn long after the life of the film. So, the essences: a series of shots that summarised the three years of work on the film, underscoring its ambition, frustrations, leg work, and the search for truth. The story was in the shots; how you could follow the entire film by studying the light rather than the narrative and still reach the same conclusions: the dirt of the fields, and in the shade of overgrown wild grass, a dead hare rotting inside a forgotten trap; the unrelenting grey of the factory with its absence of natural light, draining all colour from those who worked inside; how the sunlight caressed Lymie's sleeping head through the slats in the barn roof, and that same light bathing Spud's hand as he climbed up the ladder to reach him, his whole body emerging from shadow as if reborn by the wonder of what he saw. For many years I'd wanted to make a silent film, influenced by Jean Vigo's *L'Atalante*, which seduced my teenage mind, but the idea was discouraged by Gabi who did not believe that we could secure funding for it. In all aspects, the film we watched in the projector room was the silent film I never made: its preponderance on absence and what remained unsaid between Lymie and Spud as they canned vegetables side by side at the farm factory; the passing of boxes back and forth as they loaded up a delivery van; their knees knocking together in the cabin as Spud drove over a road littered with potholes; the arch of his back in the rear-view mirror as he pulled over to take a piss, a flash of skin around his hips and arse as his T-shirt rose up. The history of friendship in a series of shots; a rejection of family and all that was expected of them. The grotesque spectacle of the dinner table at Spud's house groaning with food when Lymie visited: of gluey mashed potatoes blending into its off-white serving platter, overcooked greens pooled in their cooking liquor, and canned corn tumbled into a bowl, a fruit jug filled with potato chips, and a coffee pot to serve the gravy. The smile Spud drew across his mash with his fork in an attempt to make Lymie comfortable; the clotted gravy as it swamped those pronged grooves. A football thrown back and forth between them across a dewy field at dawn; near-frozen breath and rosy cheeks. The trail their game left across the fallow field as one tackled another. The solidity of physical contact, Lymie jumping atop Spud as if he were a monument about to take leave. A close-up on Lymie's face as they kissed in the empty factory, heads banging against locker-room doors; less about the sensuality of touch, but more the rapture on his face afterwards, as a puzzle long struggled with became unlocked. Spud curled inwards as he was beaten in a fight he instigated against a bullying farmhand, his body becoming smaller as a fist pounded into his head and ribcage, a boot swinging back and forth into his stomach. A pool of blood on the ground as it soaked into porous stone. Spud's broken lips as he kissed a town girl in rejection of Lymie, the determination of his tongue; the latter's face across the dancefloor, how he was able to both keep still and inwardly destruct, everything communicated in the eyes. Spud's shirt being washed in the sink after the night out with his girl; Lymie's hands soaping the collar and rinsing it clean while lover boy slept it off. Hands that pulled the levers to seal cans. The same hands, later, pulling off the other's clothes in an outbuilding behind the factory. Then a refusal to kiss coinciding with the reappearance of the girl. A punch thrown by Spud's hand. The colour that bloomed across Lymie's eye socket and cheekbone. The pain of opening his eyes, and the same agony in keeping them closed. Resting on his bed with his hand across his face. The torture of his shaking frame. Finally, his profile as he sat on the edge of the factory roof, the wonder of his youth in the setting sunlight and the strength in his frame as he stood up in profile, preparing to jump. It was not Tom who cried, but Lorien as he watched the final scene play out. This is different to the rough cut, he said. It was choppier before. You kept focus on Tom's face rather than what happens around him. It felt like the truest interpretation, I said. It's so pure it breaks your heart, he said, looking at Tom with wonder. And I hadn't seen that take before. Never knew you even shot it that way. Did you never talk about it? I asked. No, said Tom, losing the mask that clouded him for the film's final reel. That's the last thing I want to talk about. He stood up and hugged me. Thanks for using that take, maestro. Didn't think you would. Thought I was crying too much. If we hadn't shot that last take I would've had nothing to compare it to, I said. I would've used one of the previous takes and told myself that the power of your agony was what you held in reserve. I didn't ask you to let go of that reserve in the scene, but you did, and everything in your loss of control made sense. It's the only way I could imagine Lymie killing himself, said Tom, he allowed himself the luxury to cry, really cry, because he knew that he would never have the opportunity again. Oh, said Lorien. Ah, that really got me. He pulled Tom hard into his chest. You need to warn me before you says things like that. It fucking kills me. Ah. I pointed to the sink in the corner. Dry your eyes, the pair of you, and splash some water on your faces. I need you to be movie stars again for Q&A if you're ready for that. We are, said Tom, nodding resolutely. Lorien gave his assent also, standing up and smoothing back his hair and then Tom's. They seemed equipped with a new understanding of themselves and what they were selling, maturing again in the two-hour running time, and somehow shining even brighter because of it. *Andiamo*, maestro, Tom said, smiling broadly. Let's go give them what they want.

11.

It was long after midnight, and having left our celebratory drinks at the palazzo, I walked the streets with Cosima, ostensibly to escort her home, though we both knew it would entail a circuitous route. Walking was the physical effort I gave to make sense of the day. It unknotted problems I spent too long entangled within and mediated in feuds I harboured. When there was no case of either, it simply embellished my satisfaction with life: walking the lanes around my home while my husband and child slept; dawn visits to film locations, needing in some way to commune with the space alone, and in doing so confirming my choices. I was pleasantly intoxicated rather than wildly drunk, wanting to preserve the feeling I'd felt on leaving the auditorium after the Q&A, one of triumph and deeply rooted contentment that my vision had been understood. I had sometimes struggled to hear that in the past, and was only at this grand age learning to pin my ears back and listen to what was actually being said. You have to realise that others do not have your vocabulary, my husband once astutely commented. If someone shakes your hand and tells you how moved they were by your film, accept that. If another recognises your reference to a shot from *Les Enfants du Paradis*, be grateful that they noticed rather than obsess about whether their tone was patronising. Learn to accept praise when it comes, no matter from whom or from which corner. You'll never stop running if you don't. I was no longer running now, just a walker enjoying the city's streets. You're happy, said Cosima. You can't stop grinning. When something goes perfectly, you have to recognise that, I said. It was what I was thinking about just now. I suppose the only sadness is that my husband wasn't here to share it with me, but we have an agreement about these events: that I can go alone and give myself fully to everything that's required, so long as I do the same when I'm at home with the family. He sounds like a clever man, said Cosima. He is, I agreed. He doesn't settle for half measures; makes me see all that I pretend to be blind to. You never mention his name, she said. I keep wondering whether you presume I know it, or if there's another reason. It's another of those pacts we made, I said. In withholding his name, I keep something for myself away from film. He's a novelist too, so if you know his name, you know his name, but it's not how I talk about myself publicly. Same with my son. You must think me strange, the more you get to know me. Not at all, she said. You fought for the freedom to marry your husband in your home country. You probably had to endure all manner of hatred to reach that point, and still here you are, travelling the world with a wedding band on your finger, and living your creative life. Make all the strange rules you want. You've earned it. We sat in a small square that ran parallel to one of the main shopping streets. There was still activity at this hour, belying its status as a minor city. Everything would close down shortly, but for the minutes remaining, locals and tourists filled their time in transit from one bar to another, arguing over cabs, or searching for places to be alone. I took Tom around a square a little like this one, I said. It had nothing special about it aside from a military statue, but the atmosphere around it was unique, as if you were leaving your bubble behind to enter a more temperate space. This has the same feeling. It's Italy, she laughed. They knew what they were doing when they built these squares: they meant to seduce you. For all my frustrations with the neighbourhood and how the city is run, I couldn't live any-where else. It can be parochial, petty and insular, but I know it like the back of my hand. Did you ever live abroad? I asked. She nodded. In Paris for a year after the novel came out. What a cliché, right? But I had a good relationship with the woman who ran the publishing house there. She could see I wasn't in a healthy place and gave me an opportunity to write for a year in the apartment she'd bought for her daughter, who was away studying in America. And how did you find Paris? I asked. Liberating to be out of the country, she said. The streets were just as narrow and crowded, but they were different people, who insulted you in an unfamiliar language when you stumbled in their way. I was breathing in their insults and the sour odour of the Metro, but it was a rush that made me feel alive, reminding me of all I could do if I put my mind to it. Such as writing, I suggested? Not quite, she said. What it killed was the idea that I could make it as a writer of fiction. I realised that I didn't have the appetite for it. How I wanted to express myself in a way that didn't involve lying. Come on! I said, novels are one of the most truthful forms there are. You proved it yourself with your book. Just because you're successful once doesn't mean that you can be again, she said. You have to really want it, that constant need to live in your head. What my time in Paris taught me was that I wanted a more direct form of expressing myself. I walked around because sitting at a desk became oppressive, and I ended up spending a lot of time looking at paintings. Graffiti again, but also old works that people had forgotten about or knew nothing of. A painting tucked away in the inner courtyard of an architect's office or decorating the staircase of an obscure restaurant. So I started writing about those. I wasn't looking to be a journalist or critic; I wanted something outside of that space. But the act of looking at a painting for a few hours and then exploring that in a piece of writing gave me more pleasure than attempting fiction again. You found your metier, I said. I didn't doubt myself in the same way, she said. I knew nothing, but somehow I was sure of myself. It was also another way to keep me close to Bruno, and I embraced that. You taught each other, I said. Not really, she replied. We knew nothing about the history of art, or about other painters. We'd just walk around until we saw a statue or painting that stopped us in our tracks. The fresco of the Virgin's ascension in the Duomo being one. We walked in there to get out of the rain one afternoon, a little high from smoking weed he bought from the caretaker's son. Aside from graffiti, and a Modigliani postcard I used as a bookmark, it was the first piece of art that left us both speechless at the same time. Something shared. Neither of us was religious outside of what was beaten into us during childhood. He was a little better than me, accompanying his mother to church on feast days, name days, and every other Sunday. It makes Mama happy, so I do it, I remember him saying. I'm nothing to shout about, but you should see the pride on her face as she holds on to my arm when we walk in. You'd think I was a big shot. His mother really was proud of him, you know? He liked his pot, but he was a good kid. We thought we were being rebellious, and we were, but by today's standards it all seems rather timid now. Painting a wall, and not going to church. Were you the same? I wasn't a revolutionary but I did my part, I said. Actually, I'm being tough on myself. Going to film school was the bravest thing I did. To say to my parents that I wasn't going to work in the same factory as my father once school had finished. That I wanted a career making films. No one at the time understood that it was even a job. It seems like a quiet revolution now, but at the time it caused fissures. My father stopped speaking to me and my brothers became cruel, protecting themselves from the rejection they imagined would happen later if I went through with it. And you're close now? she asked. We were, I said. I was as proud of them as they were of me, even if they were still bemused by it. They thought I must have fooled someone to give me money to make these films. But they saw everything when it came out and boasted to their friends, which was their way of showing approval. There's no one around now, though. Bad health took them all. I was ten years younger than my brothers. They all worked in the factory from sixteen. Their future was set from then. We sat there and reflected on our respective ghosts. It's one of the reasons my production company is based in my home town, I said. To prove to my family that it's possible to make films there and build something they thought only belonged in more sophisticated countries. Do you still feel that you have something to prove? she asked. Because the look on your face is a restless one. You've just been lauded for your film and still you're restless? Both states can coexist, I laughed. If I thought I no longer had anything to prove I wouldn't be making films. Giving up means that you know all that there is to know. On the contrary, I feel I know less the older I get. Start the first day on a new film bumbling like an amateur. This has been a thirty-year apprenticeship, with no end in sight. Don't you feel that with your writing? Less so, she said. I have to have a degree of confidence otherwise the work goes nowhere. Working your way into the heart of a painting is like solving a mystery, reaching the part that's unknown. What I rely on is the knowledge that I can string a sentence together, and that another one will roll out from it. Digging out what I need to know one line at a time. And the rest of your writing? I asked. Your project about the murals and the house? That's all unknown, she said. All these pages I've written and I still feel like I'm in the dark. You know more than other people, I said. You were there as the murals were planned and made. Oh, I have the insight, she said, but not the language. I sit at my desk and feel stuck for words. Once I finish this book I'll never write of that time again, so finding the right weight and the correct language to describe the murals is what takes time. I'm wary of sounding starstruck or not knowledgeable enough. The second-guessing you have to do as a woman writing about art. Find me a man who says he tortures himself in the same way, and I'll show you a liar. There are enough books written by those who know nothing of their subjects, just the arrogance that they're entitled to do it. This is what I'm up against when I look at the pages stacked on my desk. You must have the same feeling with all the footage you shoot for your films, or are you too much of a man to admit it? The process has a different rhythm, I said. Obviously, we're under time constraints of one kind or another, so you're less inclined to let your mind wander. Also, I'm sitting with Stjepan in the editing room as we review all the rushes, so there is no space for introspection. It can be donkey work, loading everything on to the Avid suite, logging everything and then piecing it together. Also, we have the script, which imposes a degree of structure, even if you later throw it out the window. The true freedom comes when you shoot the scenes because the flesh-and-blood responses of the actors are unknown. There could be a scene with hardly any dialogue, that says, they walk, or, they kiss, and it's in those spaces that you find what you don't expect. Those are the moments when you understand how little you know. About making films? she asked. About everything, I said. The trick is to keep doing it. The process can be an ecstatic one, even if you're walking in the dark. We left the square and walked up a hill further away from the main road. It was quieter now; moving from late to dead of night, aware of a sleeping city that had made us its guardians. Did you walk the streets like this in Paris? I asked. I tried to, but it became too difficult, she said. More than any other city, it's where men feel they can roam freely at all hours and without impunity. If it wasn't general street harassment, I'd get stopped by men who thought I was a prostitute. A hooker with punk make-up and ripped jeans. Not particularly attractive, but still selling sex in a niche way. Some cities are worse than others, I said, though that doesn't excuse the unwanted attention. It barely scratches the surface, she said. One of the reasons I think of Paris as a failure was because of how it hindered my ability to walk. I found a new direction with the paintings, and I'm grateful for that, but having to think twice about whether I should be out late at night was a bummer. A bummer? I laughed. That's right. She smiled. I was a young kid with a brattish vocabulary to match. We stood at the top of the steps looking down at the pedestrianised hill we'd climbed, breathless but exhilarated by our effort. The city lights below flickered and glowed, and beyond that was the water's gloss. The silence at this height was rarefied and as cooling as the air that stroked our faces. Where are we? I asked. The old bourgeois district, she said, though most of the old families have moved further out. Now they're apartments for their kids or their mistresses. It feels so peaceful, I said, and not just because we're so far from the main road. The rich sleep soundly, she said. I'm sure that it's the same in your city. The elevation's stunning, I said, incredulous that I'd never been here before. We were just talking about Paris, and suddenly we're in Montmartre. Montmartre without the sex pests, she laughed. Sure, there's bastards everywhere, but I won't be intimidated on these streets. Never so. I took a photo to show my husband, seduced by the cityscape and the darkness of night, before taking further photos of the cobbles, the steps and the houses that flanked us, grand mansion blocks maintained with care. I knew then that the next film would be shot entirely at night, needing to capture this sound and feel: our steps on the path as we walked further, a stray dog on the other side of the road lifting his head from a torn trash bag to study us, before continuing with his business. The protagonist from Cosima's novel walking the corridor of her apartment block at night, shopping and cooking after dark, drawing under lamplight, crying under stars. I thought of the murals through darkness and how they could be used. I wanted a sense of claustrophobia and an unravelling within a secret world. Only as she prepares to leave the university is she bathed in sunlight, filled with possibility and a sense of renewal. I'm losing you, Cosima said. You're stuck in a daydream. Sorry, I said. Got caught up. Are you still thinking about what the woman said at the Q&A? she asked. Because no one felt she had the right to talk to you like that. I'm not special, I said. People should feel free to address me in the way that they feel comfortable. If they have a strong argument, let them make it known. She was a rude bitch and she knew it, said Cosima. The smirk on her face when they handed her the microphone. She knew what she was doing. She felt that I didn't have the right to be so liberal with Maxwell's novel, I said, and she's entitled to have that view. Did she have to be so nasty about it? Cosima asked. Raising her voice like that? There was a special atmosphere in the auditorium as the film ended. Like, we were all in a collective daze, almost having to check with each other that the film was as enriching as we'd individually believed. You came down a few minutes later, so you wouldn't have seen how the room was completely silent, aside from a few who were crying here and there. It felt like a group hug after having our emotions torn to shreds and then pieced together again, only for her to pick apart that feeling with her complaints. She's the American lady who runs the English-language bookshop, I said. She comes to all my events. I respect her, even if I disagree with her opinion. I know who she is also, and I still say that she's sour, no matter how divine

her book store is, said Cosima. There's complaining from
your seat, and then there's rushing to the front of the stage
to confront you. I know the mic wasn't working properly,
but there was no need for her aggression. We'd just seen
self-aggression of the worst kind on screen with poor Lymie.
We needed someone to be tender with us, not this ranting.
I only saw passion, not aggression, I said. I knew her, don't
forget, so I didn't think she wanted to do me harm. You
were distracted, she said, by whatever went on before you
came down for the Q&A. I don't know you that well, but I
recognised the strain on your face. I was moved by my film,
I said, and by my actors' reaction to it. I'm still living with
the story as hard as I'm trying not to. After another month
of screenings my armour will be up, but I'm not there yet.
You were still talking as she walked down, so I'm not sure
whether you noticed what happened with your actors,
Cosima said. I'm not sure what you mean, I replied. Lorien
getting up to stand in front of you. How he moved so
quickly. Jumped from his chair to block her view. It was
incredible. His instinct to protect you. If someone did that
for me I'd never let them out of my sight. But I had seen.
What I remembered was a strangled sound coming from
Tom in warning before the woman ran down to the front
row. The cry in his throat registering louder than the complaints bombarding me: who did I think I was to pull apart
a classic for my own ends? That it was sadly inevitable for a
European auteur to demolish American literature and still
have the arrogance to claim to be protecting it. It was a

response to this that I was trying to clarify in my mind as Lorien stepped forward, looking at the woman and then at me. Tom then also stood, shakily, but whether that was to do with me or Lorien I didn't know. It was how Lorien disabled her that saved it, Cosima said. Holding out his hand to shake hers and smiling that movie-star smile. I didn't think she was simple enough to fall for that, considering how riled she was, but there you are. All it took was a handshake and some personal attention for her to back down. It usually does, I laughed. Having an actor around with that level of charisma gets you out of some tight spots. I spoke with more lightness than I felt, because the woman's attack had struck a note I'd intended to bury. In making this and other films, no one had ever questioned my right to tell a story and present it in the way that sang to me. I was criticised for being pretentious, whimsical, funereal, a flash in the pan, a pretender, a cine-faggot and a bore, but my right to author the stories I filmed, whether they came from my mind or other source material, was not torn apart in the same way. I did not have a literal mind when it came to adaptation and I thought that was clear, as well as how I tortured myself to show truth in all things. But that did not bury my own reservations regarding how my treatment would be received. I'd hoped that in watching the film, the audience would reach for Maxwell's novel and find comfort in the convergence of tone, rather than in setting and incident. The bones of the story were there in both if you were happy to look, but equally could be taken on their own terms. That the bookseller was outraged by the degree of separation was a criticism I would always remember because I had already flogged myself with that branch. If I were a cleverer man, I would have gone to small-town Illinois and shot the film in a more literal adaptation, with a bigger budget and cast, and a further pool of collaborators and stakeholders. I would have called upon four cameras instead of one, and a lighting rig powerful enough to grow crops from seed. But I was not that kind of director and those were the films I was incapable of making. The thought that someone interested in my work would leave the cinema disappointed in me was an unbearable one, if I only measured my satisfaction against a yardstick of crowd-pleasing. In the same way that my husband loved and accepted me for my failings, as my son would one day learn to do, I required the same of the audience. Celluloid immortalised human weakness, both in front of and behind the camera, and I hoped that was apparent. Where do we go from here? I asked. Is there a bar open, or are you ready to sleep? There's one I know close to my apartment, she said, but it's a fifteen-minute walk from here. Do you have the legs for it? We may have to steal bicycles before we get there, but let's try, I said. I'm warning you now, maestro, one nightcap and I'm done, she said. We both have busy days tomorrow. I've stopped thinking of them as separate days, I said, just one long state of being that's punctuated by nightfall. I was thinking of the new film again and my reasoning for a permanent darkness. There was no bicycle, but a child's scooter abandoned in the gutter between two parked cars. Cosima shook the dirt off the scooter and held it aloft. Dare we? she asked. We can take turns. One street length each. It looks like a death trap, I said. I'm picturing one of us with either a broken ankle or a head injury. Everything's fixable, she cried, already on it, and fast creating distance between us. Don't be timid, maestro! Her voice carried down the street and beyond; a carefree *flâneuse* no longer mindful of those she woke. The scooter's wheels squeakily laboured over the cobbles, with Cosima's posture and pace keeping her upright, only stopping when she reached the end of the street. That's incredible! she shouted. Ridiculous, but incredible! You must have a try! We're going to wake people with our shouting, I said on reaching her, which she rejected with a shrug. They're all on sleeping pills here, she said. I told you that the rich sleep soundly. Now stop trying to distract me, I can see what you're doing! Get on this, and I'll catch up with you at the bottom of the next street. You can't be serious, I said. Of course I'm serious, maestro! If you get a good speed going, you can feel the breeze! Come on, when was the last time you did something spontaneous? Like, jump in the pool with your clothes on, or throw a plate out of the window? I've never done those things, I said, knowing my rebellion to be a manufactured one, loaded on to film. My whole life had been spent living inside my head before the arrival of my family shook me out of that stupor. You couldn't be a parent to a young child without the ability to make yourself foolish for their pleasure, and it was this thought that made me feel the weight of the handle bars in my palms, as I pushed my right foot behind me in striding movements and set off. I crouched slightly in order to maintain a steady grip, making my path more zigzag than Cosima's, but once I found my rhythm, I matched her in speed. The breeze pushing past my face and into my chest was immeasurable, discomforting in the way of a soft punch, but one that I quickly grew accustomed to. I was halfway down another mansion street that led to a main road. There was no traffic noise, only the sound of the wheels shuddering over the cobbles, and the sound of my heartbeat drumming in my chest. I felt the blood pumping through my ears blocking out all other sounds; the whoops I made echoing in my head as if they were unable to escape past my interior and into the wider world. Cosima was running behind me to keep up, and as I reached the intersection, I knew that I would not give way as we agreed, pushing forward over the clear main road, and down the parallel street, a residential alley of small shops with apartment buildings above. Hey, bastard! Slow down! Maestro, bastard! Hey! I laughed through the insults and pushed harder. In reality I couldn't have been travelling that fast, the street was smoothly paved now, but with a slight incline up towards the Duomo, but I felt like I was travelling light years across the city. Catch up, Cosima, I taunted. If you want the scooter back you'll have to sprint for it! I stopped at the Duomo, exhausted, but enjoying the pain of every breath drawn. I hadn't pushed my body like that outside of the gym for a while, a reminder that I was muscle, blood and bone. Cosima looked ready to murder when she finally reached me, walking now, because she'd seen that I'd stopped and was done with running. I'm happy that you got into the spirit of it, she said, but you're still a bastard. When I get some air in my lungs I might be able to laugh about it, but not yet. When she finally reached me she grabbed the scooter with one hand and smacked the top of my head with the other. Where's this bar? I asked. You think I'm going to buy you a drink after that? she said, smiling now. If the Duomo was still open, I'd dunk your head in the font. I need a cigarette, I said, feeling the tightness now across my chest and back; the punishment those muscles would give me tomorrow. Only if you want to kill yourself, said Cosima. Breathe some clean air and give thanks that I don't punch your arm. You'd get bruises like you've never seen. She was still red in the face but there was a younger air about her as she sat on the upper steps, breathless and carefree. I thought of her running the same streets with Bruno, an exhilaration of a more intense kind, but still this lightness and possibility of hope. What takes this away and what rekindles the flame? She had created a life for herself, and if there was joy, was there enough of it? The times my husband and I laughed at the antics of our child; daily laughter, always surprising and unconfined, and I felt guilty for thinking about it at that moment, self-conscious of those images being at the forefront of my memory; its importance greater than anything else I had achieved. I did not judge whether my joy was greater than her joy, or where the disparity lay, if any. She had one up on me for forcing me into the scooter ride; without that I would have remained a city drunk stumbling the route home. What she'd given me was a stripping back of years, when I was freer in body and mind. You have the look of someone who wants to judge me, but you don't have the right, she said. Where did that come from? I asked. The look on your face, she said. You're a man, so you make it too obvious. It's a look I see all too often. The way men look at women who are not wives or mothers. If you didn't have your family I still wouldn't look at you with the impunity that you stare at me now. You think that you're able to because you're a film director. That having a vocation means that you can intrude so long as you learn something new about human nature and replicate it with your film camera afterwards. It makes me wonder how much of your films are real and what part of them consists of stolen moments, where you saw real life happening before your eyes and decided that you would use it somehow. Have you ever written a film simply based on a look your saw or a scene you witnessed? A child crying in the street because he dropped his ice cream or a couple on a train having a row about politics that developed into something more serious? Or the reactions of the people around you after an old man is knocked down in the street? Many times, I said, but this isn't one of those. I don't believe you, she said. This is what your precious imagination boils down to: stealing and hoarding. Don't get me wrong, I'm not naive enough to think that the history of art is a pure one. Like cinema, it's a story of

insecurity, rivalry and theft. But I didn't expect to be thinking the same of you. Not that you're on a pedestal, just I
thought that you had greater sense. I'm still confused as to
how I'm meant to be looking at you, I said. I thought we
were having fun with the scooter. Is it because I took off and
left you to walk all that way? Don't do that, she said. Try to
deflect your guilt by asking questions. There's a reason you're
not an actor, maestro. Your feelings are too close to the
surface. I saw the look on your face out of the corner of my
eye as I was catching my breath. You pretty much appraised
and summarised my life with that one look, and I didn't
deserve that. Everything I told you about women walking
the streets, of the freedom to do so this late at night precisely
to avoid the gaze of judgemental men, that's to say, all men.
What gave you the right? Do you look at Lorien this way?
Or Tom? You're right, I said, and I don't. Not at them. But
you'd steal from them, though? she asked. If you felt you had
just cause? I don't steal from anyone, I said. I don't create
fantasies. My films are rooted in real life; therefore I'm influenced by what's around me. Ha! You make it sound so gentle
and unknowing with your use of 'influence', she said. Jails
are packed with those who've been touched by influence.
Just because you put your influences on the screen and light
it well, you expect to always get away with it. Well, I see
through that, maestro. I see through you! The brutality of
her analysis cut me to the core, itself a reprisal for the look
I had indeed given her and immediately regretted, but rather
than owning up, I insisted on this pantomime to protect

myself instead of apologising to her. When my husband had confronted me about my behaviour in this same city all those years ago, with his accusations of distance and the same look that I had given Cosima, I hid behind rhetoric, taking apart his words because I thought I was able; forgetting that he wrote novels so could twist my words back in a way that left me unstuck. Never get into arguments with writers! Stop lying and apologise, he said simply. If you're unable to do that, then we're both wasting our time. And when I was unable to say anything, too consumed with a sense of false injustice, he turned and walked away. If I had to identify a true moment of influence, one that would shape the next decade and beyond, it was the sharp pain of seeing someone potentially slip away that I did not wish to lose. Similarly, the fear, wonder and absolute love on being present at the birth of my child. These were the moments I wanted to define and inform me, rather than the egotism of before. But still I lapsed, thinking that I had a greater right to mine the experience of those around me than those people them-selves, all because I had the tools. Cosima had seen right through it and would not let up until I confessed. You're right in everything you say, I told her. I don't have the right but I still expect to get my way. It's been like this for so long, I need reminding that it's not the accepted way to treat people. I'm an idiot, and those who are close expect it of me. That remains a poor excuse, she said. The ability to recog-nise when you're at fault does not give you licence to continue. I'm aware of that, I said. I'm trying. I'm wondering now whether that woman was right in her attack on you earlier, she said. The American bookseller. What gave you the notion to mess around with the book as you saw fit? The same right as any artist, I said, feeling on safer ground. It's the ability to present a perspective challenging an established view that defines art, no? Even when it's wrong? she asked. Just so, I said. It's the existence of the viewpoint that matters, whether you disagree with it or not. Should I have waited until someone had filmed a more standard adaptation of Maxwell's book before making my version? When you're filled with passion for a project, obsession even, you can't afford to wait. Do you believe that the woman was right to say what she did? asked Cosima. Or is your decision ultimately greater than hers? If she feels that strongly, I said, maybe she should go and make the film herself. You're so arrogant, she said. I can't believe I hadn't noticed that before. I have the right to produce the film I have in my mind, I said. Of course you do, she replied. I just wonder whether that's the case with someone else's story. I'm cutting to the chase to save us another day of dancing around each other. I wouldn't be comfortable allowing someone to film my novel if their approach was similar to *The Folded Leaf.* It used to be a dream of mine, to have a film made, until I think about that bookseller's anger. As much as it was a rant at you, it served as a warning to me. So you're thinking about whether your novel can be made into a film, I said, smiling. How did we get on to this topic? You can stop that, she said. Don't try to be charming when I'm still angry with you.

The book is at the top of your pile, and not just because you had such a strong reaction to it. I imagine Gabrijela is rushed off her feet with meetings and other business at the festival, yet she had time to start reading my book on the day of your premiere. Why would that be unless you were considering it? All that came to you from Gabi's passing comments about the book? I asked. She looks at everything, if that makes you feel better. The best producers are those with curious minds, and she likes to know what's out there. I spoke to Stjepan, too, she said. He told me that Gabrijela had a sense that this was capturing your attention over everything else, and that he should prepare. You read my book last night and already this is happening? This is how it works, I wanted to tell her. When one idea starts to take precedence over others I let myself be consumed by it. I'll work through the night and not sleep; entering an anxious state of being until my plans become concrete and a shooting schedule set. I'll live with the characters and play out their roles. I'll flesh out the back stories of everyone who speaks in the film, even if it is no more than one line, enabling me to give the actors the notes they require when their intuition is lost. I'll take photographs using differing sources of natural light, and send these back and forth with my cinematographer. Sometimes I'll need a picture with the correct lighting before I can even start on the script. Other times it can be an object, such as a scarf or a fork from my mother's cutlery set; a photograph or object to set the tone for what I want to create. Cosima was only half right: cinema was concerned with the story, but equally it could have nothing to do with it. What made it on to film involved a second sight that sometimes had little to do with what was on the page, but was more down to atmospherics, with their own rules and complications, no more so than in my determination to piece together a vision through chaos. I wanted you to write the film with me, I said. I mean, that's what I was going to ask. Once I was sure. OK, she said, after a series of long exhalations; the drawing of breath pushing down her anger and replacing it with a colder scrutiny. I wasn't expecting that, maestro. But that still doesn't excuse how you looked at me. You don't get to judge my life just because you might want to make a film together. It's the book you're putting on the screen, not the person behind it. Is that how you look at the paintings? I asked. Do you take them purely on their own terms, or are you looking for signs of the hand that created them? It's both and you know it, she said. That still doesn't entice me to succumb to the same rigour. Writing a book that you like doesn't make me a commodity, or have you spent so long in theft that you don't know the difference? Splicing parts of one man's personality to fit another, and then one more after that, to produce the construct that best suits your films. How do I know that half my words won't be chopped, or that you'll make more drastic changes? This is the gamble of all films, I said, for myself as much as for those I collaborate with. The plan is to know, but the rush comes from not knowing, right up to the final edit. My instinct is not to gamble, she said, because I know what it can do to me. I see how devoted you are with your actors. Is this a way to keep them close to you, by offering up this film? Tom playing the grieving girl, and Lorien as the tenant upstairs? I'm not judging your desires, just saying that what's obvious to me may be even clearer to those who know you better. Do you want me to tell you truth, or what you want to hear? I asked. For I'm too old to spin you a line. There are no guarantees, Cosima. All I can promise is to treat your book with the same respect as I give to the finished film. The two won't match, for I'm not a natural matchmaker, but there will be sense in it, feeling and truth. But not my truth, she said. This is what I realise now. My vision exists solely on the page, and if I'm egotistical enough to want to see it expanded on to film, I must compromise to my detriment. That's as clear a summary as I know, I said. That's what makes you a writer, your ability to get to the heart of the argument. You see that, don't you? What an asset you would be on the project? I can't do it, maestro, she said. Did you ever think to ask me if I had dreams to adapt and film the book myself? I may not have your facilities, a studio in my backyard, and a team to execute my plans, but that doesn't mean that I can't wish it. You were so wrapped up in telling my story, that you didn't ask yourself whether my need to protect that story was greater. In many ways it breaks my heart, because I had visions of us being great friends. At this age when you meet someone you connect with so quickly, it's a gift you shouldn't deny. I've shared more about myself with you in two days than I have to friends I have known for much longer. Yet here I am rejecting it. We felt like strangers now; martyrs from different religious factions unwavering in their beliefs. We had both lost the elation of before, avoiding the other's gaze because to do so was to confirm the schism, and some part of me hoped that it was not past repair. I could not turn my back on the novel with the plans for the film being so fresh in my mind. I was alive to all its possibilities and con- flicts, wanting to find a compromise that did not feel like it was so. I was certain that if I did not make this film then I would never do so again, so strong was my desire to create from all I had learned. Cosima had given voice to the rarity of our friendship also, and the prediction that this too would end stung as sharply as the night air burning my cheeks. There was still a space for me to apologise but no words would come; locked and unable to project. I valued our rapport and the ease in which we walked together, but I did not wish to insult her further by lying. The walks were important to me. I imagined doing the same in New York if the film was shown there, or reclaiming Paris back from the legions who'd harassed her. The kilometres our feet would cross; ring roads and waterways, every church and monument. I thought of her sitting across the table from my husband and child, and whether they would see the qualities that made her such good company. How she would fit into the production team overseen by Gabrijela; if a place could be found for her to excel. The ebb and flow of contrasting voices as we worked on the script, whether harmony blos- somed over mistrust and disagreement; whether I had the

ability and willingness to see through her eyes. It was infat-
uation of a different sort, one that would morph into a more
regular friendship in time. For now I wanted to keep picking
the bones for all remaining flesh from her story, because
there was truth in the contrary view: that the story was more
important than she was, and I would do what it took to
secure it. I was not brave enough to give voice to that, but
it existed in the darkness of how films were formed. If I said
you could write the whole script without interference, what
would you say? I asked. To present the script and allow me
to shoot it. She looked at me for a long while before she
spoke, as both of us remained frozen in place on the steps.
Her face made my failure clear, and how our futures flashed
before us, illusory and without principle. She could never
live that way. I think that you'll tell me anything in order
to get the film made, she said, standing up. Just the fact of
you making that offer confirms that I can't trust you, and
that's sadder than anything to do with a book I wrote thirty
years ago. Really sad. I'll make my own way home from
here, maestro. Thank you for reading my work, but I can't
see you again.

12.

I was restless on arriving back at the palazzo, circling my room in a series of stumbling laps, as if trapped by my arrogance and weakness of mind. I felt wounded and sorry for myself, but mostly in a state of deep unease, knowing that something previously undefined had been uprooted and left to survive at will. I remember the shock of my parents passing one after another within the space of six months, and how I spent that time barely sitting down, as if by pacing I would better process the information. It pained me to think of the distress I had caused Cosima, damage which went far beyond our parting on the Duomo steps; how something of that moment would be carried into her writing and either further her engagement with the world or initiate a withdrawal from it. The blame lay utterly with me for the way in which I had let her down. Equally, I was desperate about the film, feeling the ache of a parting summer romance, for a still-embryonic idea that continued to sit inside my jacket pocket. It was so precious I felt barely able to touch it, but still I needed it to exist outside my head and in my hand. I would have paced for the rest of the night, had I not had a visitor. I can't sleep, said Tom. Can I come in? He had the face of a child: screwed-up with tiredness, but believing himself not to be. Dressed in one of Lorien's tracksuits now, his odour was purely bed and the man who'd possessed him. I tried calling earlier but it kept ringing out, he continued, walking through the suite and jumping on to the couch. He took very little interest in his surroundings, only in as much as finding the most comfortable spot in which to drift; padding in the manner of the family cat, preparing his bed. I presumed you were still out with the graffiti lady. Cosima, I corrected. That's who I meant, he said. She's nice, I like her. I thought you'd be with Lorien, I said. I was, but he's sleeping now, said Tom. It's strange. I've never felt as safe as I do lying next to him. Within him, even. His arms are around me and I think, This is what it means to feel safe in the world. But I still can't sleep, at least not for long. So you thought you'd keep me awake, is that it? I asked. I'll go back there shortly. I just wanted to give him a couple of hours without me fidgeting in bed. Is it weird me talking to you about this stuff? I'm just thinking that if I can't get to sleep being next to Lorien, what will it take? Patience, I said, and the ability to step outside your thoughts. Do you want a chamomile tea? No thanks, he said. I'm still pissing champagne. Lorien promised to get me drunk and he delivered. I'm not feeling too bad now, though. Do you want to watch a movie? I asked. It'll probably help us both to unwind. I do, he said, nodding happily. I want to feel like we're back shooting the film with our cosy family. We only have one more day of this and then we split up again. Not so literally with you, I said, because you'll still be with Lorien. Not quite, he replied. I have a third callback in New York, and he's going straight to Montreal for a test shoot. Was supposed to be the following week, but his agent called through earlier. We won't see each other for over ten days. You'll survive a fortnight, I said. I hope so, he replied. The intensity is killing me. I'm going to show you a film from my part of the world, I said. Not quite my country, but close enough. You'll see in this what drove me to filmmaking. That's the kind of movie I can stay awake for, he said. I always want to know more about you, without knowing how to ask. Just ask, I said. It's that simple. We watched Krzysztof Zanussi's *The Structure of Crystal*. This is a two-hander mostly, I said, between two close friends, fellow physicists, who're reunited after several years apart. Finding that their life has taken different turns. It's about the philosophy of friendship and life choices. So they're like brothers, said Tom, not taking his eyes from the screen. Look at the care they're taking as they're bathing each other. It's beautiful. This is the sort of film I want to make with Lorien. Just how they're walking and driving. Talking about everything and nothing. These are the hardest scripts to find, because no one wants to make films like this any more, I said. Hold on, let me rewind this. Look at this shot again of the two of them running in the

field, and the dog joins in. Running so fast that they trip up
over her and she gives a yelp of protest. Listen to that! Look
at the surprise on their faces as it happens. Nothing to do
with the story, but just something that freely occurs in the
space when you allow the characters to be. You shoot scenes
like that now, and they want you to cut them out. I thought
our film was solely made up of scenes like that, he smiled.
Ah, but we have the element of tragedy, I said. This is what
the audience waits for. Here, there's only breathing space,
and the uncertainty of whether you're living the life meant
for you. That strikes a chord, he said, more than you know.
Check out the distance he shoots the house from, maestro,
so that you see how isolated it is in the field. Were you
thinking of that when we were in the barn? The scene where
Lymie's at the window watching Spud at work, before walking through the field to meet him. Same as this, single shot.
Clever boy, I said. No one else will notice, but the structure
of the barn reminded me a little of home. I guess I wanted
to reflect that in a very direct way. Tom's eyes were glazed
now, softly filling with sleep. I want a home, he said. With
Lorien if he'll have me. Getting drunk once a week and
watching movies. It could happen, right? Everything you
want can happen, I said. Did tonight make you happy,
maestro? he asked. Did we do you proud? Incredibly, I said.
As if you need to ask. Now they see what I see. How about
you? The happiest, he said faintly, his voice slipping. And
not just because they adore the film. I never want to lose
this. You won't, I said, understanding that he would need a

safe place to land, for the intensity of temporal joy could never be maintained. He would draw upon its destruction for his next film, the way all actors grew. Ten films from now, his face would be a battleground. Now get some sleep, I continued. I'll wake you in an hour. I watched him as he slept, for to do so took my mind away from my failures. I continued to feel unsettled by the abrupt end of my conversation with Cosima. I felt the free fall of limbo, uncertain if and when the feeling of being unmoored would cease. The easy solution would be to call her, but I knew my gesture would go unanswered. She was angry and rightly so. In her mind I was the master of gesture with no substance behind it, or more precisely, the substance of others. How much of this was right, and how much was self-pity, for I was at the hour when only this explanation made sense. To pull myself out of danger I called my husband from the bathroom. I was accused of theft earlier, I said. Does that sound right to you? Back up and explain what's been happening first, he said. I was giving myself some extra time to write because it's the weekend tomorrow and there won't be the opportunity. If you're going to interrupt that, you have to make it worth my while. Now slow down and start again. And why are you whispering? His tone softened when he heard what I had to say, my words running into each other, so keen was I to get the story out before it mutated in my mind. No matter the trouble I found myself in, he was always the first to be at my side. I continued to give daily thanks for what we had. By revealing the facts of the evening I wanted to expunge them, and to be gently reassured that my way of thinking and working could continue. To turn away from that would be to suggest that my viewpoint had been wrong for all those years; showing that what appeared to be true had corroded to artifice. In the same way that untreated film destroys itself over time, so too were my ideas, fracturing and turning black with decay. The emptiness I felt was beyond anything I'd experienced, as if discovering that half my known life had been erased. You're no thief, my husband said, but you underestimated the strength of feeling for her ideas, which isn't like you. Have you been getting enough sleep as we discussed? I can tell you haven't because I can still hear it in your voice. You shouldn't talk to me if you don't want your voice to give you away. When you get home, I'm going to lace your coffee and have you sleeping for a week. You can't keep going like this. But I've nothing to worry about, is that what you're saying? I asked. More that you need to stay calm and get some perspective, he said. If someone tried to water down your ideas in the same way you'd have their head on a stick. Why do you think we never work together? Because we're not sadists! We stay in our respective lanes. You're not confrontational, but you're fiercely protective of your territory. You must respect how others are protective of theirs. I truly thought you would've learned this by now. How often have we talked of this? But no matter. Whatever the case, let these words sink in now, but be kind to yourself about it. You're an old dog who can still learn new ways. Let go of this film, for however elevating its potential, it'll make you miserable. If this is how you are before you begin, think of your state by the time you complete it. Worth the damage, do you think? I don't know, I said. I'd like to think so. But there are no certainties, he replied. And if you're unable to secure the rights, you won't get the story you want anyway. Walk away before barriers are put up before you. It may hurt for a while, for the loss of the idea as well as your bruised ego, but you'll live. There'll be other ideas which'll grip you just as passionately. You just haven't found them yet. I did not quite agree, but neither did I put up a fight; in my slow way I was simply accepting what was. I agreed that I would return home in the morning, before the jury decision was announced. It no longer felt important, and I did not have the appetite for another party, whatever the outcome, needing the flesh-and-blood touch of my two men at home more; the solidity of holding both greater than a trophy's affirmation. Gabi would be pissed but she would find a way to make it work, as she had before. When I returned to the bedroom, Tom had left, the last minutes of the film still running. He physically felt the distance between himself and Lorien, even when it was of his own making. I marvelled at the strength of it, and wondered whether it would hold. I wished it, but knew of Hollywood's tricks. They would not be in possession of their free will once they returned. If this was my last night, I could not stay in my room with pent-up energy tearing through my insides; my thoughts unresolved. Tomorrow I would sleep for as long as my husband insisted: a day, a week;

whatever it took to restore us both. Like the reclusive phys-
icist in the Zanussi film, he wanted us to live quietly, and
for breathing space to become our way of life. It mostly was,
aside from these interludes of derailment. This I needed to
remind myself. I pulled my notebook into a bag along with
Cosima's short stories and headed for the garden, walking
the long way around the palazzo, taking me past Lorien's
room. I was aware that this was a final opportunity to be so
close to them if my husband made right on his promise to
arrange with Gabi for the earliest possible flight. I stood
outside the door for a few minutes, taking in the timbre of
their voices as they talked quietly between themselves; a
burgeoning choral sound as their tones melded, which made
me content. I pressed my fingers lightly on the door as if to
prove that it was there, and their happiness beyond, but also
to give a blessing from a faith I believed I had long since
buried. I was an atheist who still prayed for the well-being
of my child every night, and my touch blessing on their door
was of the same intention. Everything we run away from is
slowly accepted in the end. I found Stjepan smoking at a
table in the walled garden, battered but contemplative. What
are you doing up at this hour? he asked me. Wide awake, I
said. Thought I'd try to do some work. Fuck work, he said.
You've been working flat out for weeks. Have a cigarette
with me and entertain the possibility that all this is coming
to an end. What do you mean? I asked. We've reached the
finish line, he said. Not only reached, but crossed it. You
can stand still and allow your heart rate to return to normal.

For your breathing to slow. You're still at race speed, I can see it. As if it's that easy, I laughed. At this age, the body starts to do what it wants, rather than listen to what I want. Why are you still up, too? Not just waiting to give me advice, I presume? I like it here, he said. Back in Zagreb, if I wanted to sit in the garden at this hour, they'd be someone following me: wife, babies, dogs. I'm enjoying being a selfish bastard for the night. No one to comment on how much I've drunk, or how many cigarettes I've hammered. In the old days, as you well know, there might've been speed or cocaine to keep me going at one of these parties. Now I just want to end the night with a quiet smoke and perhaps a really greasy grilled cheese sandwich, which they finish in butter just to be extra fancy. This is how we wrap things up, maestro. Not with a bag of books. I've had all I can drink, but the sandwich sounds good, I said. Let's teach my body a lesson by flooding it with tar and grease. We smoked quietly, taking in the night rhythms of the garden as the breeze rang against the wrought-iron chairs, before being absorbed into the bushes; the crack of the trees themselves, and the scratch of something falling unseen, of leaves or a branch being dragged across stone. I spoke to one of the festival organisers as they were leaving the bar, he said. Plastered she was, but she's tight with one of the younger guys on the jury. The kind we like who can't keep their mouth shut. What's the word? I said, my stomach contracting. That the prize is pretty much yours unless there's strong disagreement when they meet tomorrow. There's no other film with the same level of consensus. So it's mine because they couldn't agree on anything better? I asked. He laughed. Don't be a baby. If they didn't think it was brilliant, they wouldn't even be discussing it. Only you could actually think of the trophy as a consolation prize. It's not decided yet, I said. Plenty of time for them to argue through their hangovers. Did you tell this to Gabi? No, he said. She went to bed not long after you left. The festival crew only got their cabs about an hour ago. You know what it's like. No one leaves until the bar is well and truly dry. She'll be over the moon, I said, Gabi. And how do you feel about it? he asked. You're not one to jump on tables, but it feels like one of those moments, no? Tomorrow, I said, maybe. But not until we know for sure. Is this why you're carrying these books around, he asked, to atone for something yet to happen? Not quite, I said. You talked about the finish line, and I feel truly past that. This is why I can't sleep, because I want to keep moving forward. Cosima's book, he nodded. Me and Gabi talked about it earlier. She said it had your touch written all over it. She hadn't finished it but could see its potential. I think we were both wondering why it hadn't been adapted before. The premise is pretty strong. That's down to Cosima, I said. The story behind the novel is so personal to her, I don't think she can entrust it to anyone's hands. Even yours? he asked. Even mine, I said. She made it very clear earlier. I'm not the person she thought I was, put it that way. So why are you sitting here with your books? he said. That's one of hers poking out of your bag, isn't it? Because I can't let go of the idea, I guess, I said. I'm hoping that she'll either change her mind or accept my apology. Both, preferably. What do you have to apologise for? he asked. For handling the situation badly, I said. For being boorish and too used to getting my own way. And she's right, too. This is why we keep the champagne away from you, he said, because you start to get maudlin for no reason. Since when did you care what anyone thought? You don't make films by committee, maestro. You have vision, and this is why we follow you. But what if I'm intruding on someone else's vision? I said. What purpose does that serve? You'll intrude where you have to in order to get the film you want, he said. I've worked with some Machiavellian bastards who ripped off other films or scripts and claimed them as their own without a care. You know the ones I'm talking about. They usually end up with a Palme d'Or. You're not in that league of deceptiveness, maestro, but neither are you shy of doing what you have to for the result you desire. We've cut entire characters out of the edit. Main characters! And you did it for the right reasons. Because with that one particular film, what those two actors brought to the screen was superfluous to your needs. Do you remember that day? The pair of them turning up at the studio ready to bash your head in after discovering that they were chopped? I didn't think you'd get out alive. It was wrong how we told them, I said. I shouldn't have left it so late. I knew as we were filming it that I would have to cut them out, but I wanted both to keep playing their roles anyway, to see what they would bring, especially in regards to the other actors.

I thought back to that production and how I lived as a liar for the three months of filming. Only on the first day of the assembly edit, as Stjepan and I painstakingly cut them away, scene by scene, did I begin to breathe. This was part of the process: to add, subtract, and subtract again. Film was a three-way game of chance, where your ability to create life moved from the script, to the photography, and finally the edit. I had given those characters life in two out of the three; in script and on set, I honoured them as best I could. Only in the edit was it clearer than ever that I answered to no one, gluing together a cohesive series of reels where I explained myself. The two actors understood when they saw the final shape of the film. You put us through hell, one said. You publicly humiliated us, but we see that you have a better film for it. We'll never work with you again, or forgive you for our treatment, but at least we now see the reasoning, and appreciate the logic, even if our hearts don't. Sometimes you just need to try things out, said Stjepan, even if it takes a year of your time. Longer, even. I've seen you do it before and you'll do it again, no matter how tired you pretend to be. You're one of the few I know able to finance a film yourself, shoot and edit, only to scrap the whole thing entirely if you felt it wasn't worthy to be seen. Process, maestro. Why we follow you. I knew then that I would follow this path for the film to be made. Afterwards, we'd see. Back upstairs, I turned down the sound on the television and watched the last scenes of *The Structure of Crystal*, nostalgic for a time when I was ignorant and free-willed.

Filmmaking was an adventure and would continue to be one, but without the wide-eyed naivety of before. When Zanussi made this film in 1969, his first, did he know that his ability and viewpoint would grow with subsequent films? Did he welcome that or wish to stem it? Committing to film is an act of preservation, and in every feature I made there remained an imprint of myself at that particular time; my perceived wisdom culled from the experience of shooting it, together with the imperfections at the root of my ongoing blight. What would I find of myself looking at *The Folded Leaf* a decade from now? What would I recognise and what would be alien to me? The pride I felt in the film was strong, so I knew that this would carry, but how clearly would I recognise my failings? I thought of Tom and Lorien looking at the picture at the home they might share, or away on location, alone in a room similar to this one. What would my husband share of this to others, or my son? Where would he find me in the film, and would his understanding of that be something that he carried into his adult life? Like Zanussi's brotherly physicists, like Spud and Lymie, I felt that I was standing alone in the middle of the field. Midsummer, with grasses rising high against my upper legs; the afternoon sun burning the top of head and arms. I was far from others, and still I waited to be seen.

Thank you:
Andrew Gallix, Berkeley Books of Paris,
Dennis Cooper, Edouard Louis.

ABOUT THE FONT

This book is set in Bembo, a typeface designed by punch-cutter Francesco Griffo (1450–1518) for the Venetian printer and publisher Aldus Manutius. It was first used in February 1496 for the pamphlet *De Aetna* by poet, scholar and later cardinal Pietro Bembo.

Bringing a book from manuscript to what you are reading is a team effort.

Dialogue Books would like to thank everyone at Little, Brown who helped to publish *Diary of a Film* in the UK.

Editorial
Sharmaine Lovegrove
David Bamford

Contracts
Melanie Leggett

Sales
Andrew Cattanach
Ben Goddard
Hannah Methuen
Caitriona Row

Design
Nico Taylor
Jo Taylor

Production
Narges Nojoumi

Publicity
Millie Seaward

Marketing
Emily Moran

Copy-Editor
Alison Tulett

Proofreader
Saxon Bullock